THE MISFORTUNATES

Born in Belgium in 1972, DIMITRI VERHULST is the author of a collection of short stories, a volume of poetry and several novels, including *Madame Verona Comes Down the Hill*, published by Portobello Books. In 2009 he was awarded the Libris Prize in the Netherlands.

DAVID COLMER is an Australian writer and translator. He has won several translation prizes and in 2010 his translation of Gerbrand Bakker's *The Twin* won the IMPAC Dublin Literary Award.

ALSO BY DIMITRI VERHULST

Madame Verona Comes Down the Hill

The Misfortunates

DIMITRI VERHULST

Translated from the Dutch by David Colmer

Portobello
BOOKS

Published by Portobello Books 2012

Portobello Books
12 Addison Avenue
London
WII 4QR

Copyright © Dimitri Verhulst 2007

English translation copyright © David Colmer 2012

First published in Dutch in 2007 as *De helaasheid der dingen*
by Uitgeverij Contact, the Netherlands

The right of Dimitri Verhulst to be identified as the author
of this work and David Colmer's right to be identified as its
translator have been asserted by them in accordance with
the Copyright, Designs and Patents Act 1988.

The translation of this book is funded by the
Flemish Literature Fund (Vlaams Fonds voor de
Letteren – www.flemishliterature.be).

Flemish
Literature
Fund

A CIP catalogue record is available from the British Library

9 8 7 6 5 4 3 2 1

ISBN 978 1 84627 158 8

www.portobellobooks.com

Printed and bound by CPI Group (UK) Ltd, Croydon, CR0 4YY

For Windop. And in memory of my grandmother,
who wanted to avoid the shame and died while I was
completing the last pages of the manuscript.

Any similarity between existing people
and certain characters in this book is due
solely to insight into human nature.

I was surprised that someone would devote a life to such things, to faking things and not quite succeeding at it, and when one succeeds one only adds one ephemera to another, what one can't have to what one doesn't.

Pierre Michon, Masters and Servants

Why do I no longer dream about my mother? Perhaps because I have written too much about her, even distributing her beautiful profile on the cover of a book. Without meaning to exorcize anything, I exorcized her presence. My mother wasn't bothering me, I summoned her up myself by writing so much about her, but I suspect that in the end I created a literary character – complex, artistic, complicated – and lost the real mother, the dead mother, as a result. I am the orphan of a dead mother because I wrote too much about her.

Francisco Umbral, A Creature of Distance

A Good-Looking Kid

My Auntie Rosie's supposed return to Arsendegem came as a pleasant shock in the lives of our completely useless men, whose number I was on the verge of increasing. The day opened with her name – Rosie! Rosie! – bringing hope. Because someone had come back. Someone who had been born here and had left this place had come again! And it had been Rosie! Her return was interpreted as an Old Testament sign, proof that even Arsendegem had redeeming features and we too were not as worthless as had been mathematically established.

It's true that my Auntie Rosie was an unusually beautiful woman, and having been to bed with her was a source of considerable prestige. At the height of her beauty my grandfather, who didn't have an ounce of respect for anyone who couldn't hold his booze, happily accepted round after round from brave young men who hoped to swill their way into his favour by challenging him to drinking contests, with their standing as ideal son-in-law as the stakes. By then the cancer had already metastasized all through his yardstick of a body. More and more often he needed to interrupt his phenomenal drinking sessions to go and spew blood in the toilet, and he didn't live to see his much-admired daughter finally wed. Five fathoms – apparently that's the depth to which drunkards too are lowered into the merciful earth. Until my grandmother wasted away in an old people's home, she saw it as her widowly duty to buff up his pitch-black marble slab once a week. After the funeral of her father, Our Supreme Drinker, Auntie Rosie gave herself away to a man without history and moved with him to our distant capital, much to the sorrow of our own young men, who had to content themselves with blighting the lives of uglier women. Yet again, Arsendegem saw that everything beautiful must leave or be destroyed.

Auntie Rosie wanted less and less to do with her home town; tearing herself away with the help of a man (we weren't even sure of his name, let alone his capacity for drink) must have made as much of an impression on her as a narrow escape from death. During rare telephone conversations, she talked about accumulated wealth, the bustling city, renovating the roof garden and the pleasures of a sauna. The summertime postcards she sent to keep in touch with the home front bore unimaginative, sunny greetings from remote destinations we refused to look up in the atlas. And during her even less frequent visits, we begged her husband not to park his enormously expensive car in front of the house. We were poor, always had been, but we bore our poverty with pride. A flash car in front of the house was a humiliation, and the thought that a fellow resident of Arsendegem might notice that a Verhulst had amounted to something financially was a shameful thing.

It's like this: I spent my first years with my parents in Kanton Street on a tiny courtyard with a communal water pump and a communistic toilet – a hole in a plank, directly above the septic tank. Water ran down the inside of the living-room walls and we stuffed balls of newspaper into the worm-eaten window frames to keep out the wind. My father always spoke of the inconveniences of our residence with pride – longing for an easy life was a clear sign of inadequate masculinity – and when we finally moved to Mere Street it was only to be even worse off. Our new toilet was a hole in a plank as well, but this house had the advantage of a leaking roof. Our kitchen floor was covered with buckets that caught the drops from the ceiling. We spent pleasant evenings together on the sofa listening to the well-rounded sound of splashing and trying to guess the xylophone tunes the ruined roof was playing us. We refilled the little bowls of rat poison daily: instead of exterminating the vermin, we felt like we were doing a good job of taking care of the little critters. And we cherished the rotten, mushroom-sprouting death trap of a staircase over the cellar as a prime example of proletarian architecture. My father was a socialist and went to great lengths to be recognized as such. For him, possessions were nothing more or less than extra dusting. You didn't own them, they owned you. If a burst of unexpected thrift put us in danger of reaching the end of the month with a financial surplus, he hurriedly plundered the bank account and drank his entire pay packet to protect us from the temptations of capitalism. Unfortunately my mother revealed herself more and more as a bourgeois cow: she was too vain for worn-out shoes and filed for divorce after just ten years of marriage. When she left, she took everything that wasn't nailed down, thus granting my father ultimate bliss. At last he owned nothing, neither wife nor

3

other furniture, and moved back in with his elderly mother. But this much is clear: we looked down on family members who parked their fancy cars in front of the house when they showed up in disgustingly expensive clothes to visit us on holidays.

Inimitable, the rhythm of the rumour that Rosie – miraculous! miraculous! – had returned to Arsendegem, and I spent those days being constantly buttonholed by reborn men who wanted to know if the town's drunken mouth was speaking the truth. It definitely was: to our astonishment as well, Auntie Rosie had come back with two black eyes and her head bowed, asking if she and her daughter could move in with us for a while.

'With us' meant with my grandmother. Four of her five sons, my father amongst them, had made a mess of their love life and moved back in with their mother. As my own mother was sick to death not just of my father but of me too, my grandmother had taken me under her wing and I passed the listless days together with my father and three uncles. Now we were going to be joined by my Auntie Rosie and my cousin, Sylvie, on the run from a man who tormented them with adultery and aggression.

I only saw my Brussels cousin sporadically, usually at funerals or on New Year's Day, when we sensed that we came from different worlds and wisely ignored each other. I suspected her of playing the piano and ballet dancing in pink tutus. She was the kind of girl who kept track of how many calories she put away daily and took it for granted that her Father Christmases would always have fat bank accounts. University was a certainty on her horizon, and since she'd inherited

4

her mother's beauty, she would soon be able to entertain herself by encouraging men to waste their time trying to win her over. She was a little younger than me, but gave such a self-assured impression that I didn't dare to pull seniority on her in any field at all. I was not happy about her arrival. Our male bastion had suited me just fine without her getting in the way. Sylvie's respectable upbringing got to us, and we saw the sorry state we were in reflected in her eyes.

My father always shat with the door wide open. His compost gave off an extraterrestrial stench of farmyard cheddar and he'd often stand in the hall with his clangers hanging free, six feet away from the bowl so I couldn't pretend I hadn't heard him, yelling at me to fetch a fresh bog roll and the rest of the newspaper. He'd done it like that for years and the system worked perfectly: he always got his toilet roll and something to read immediately. But now, with Sylvie watching, it was as if we suddenly needed to apologize for ourselves. We were ashamed of the way we came downstairs in the morning in our Y-fronts with a hand in under the elastic to have a good scratch. We were ashamed of how we sprawled in front of the TV puffing away with our sweaty feet up on the table. We were ashamed of the pounds of raw mince we ate because it was cheap and easy, and we were ashamed of the way we stuck our fingers into the mince to grab a handful to stuff into our mouths before washing it down with cold coffee that had been left standing in a mug from yesterday. We were ashamed of the worms we got from the mince and didn't do anything about. We were ashamed of the way we farted like bandmasters, and we were ashamed of the burps we did nothing to restrain. We were ashamed of swearing for no reason, of the pubic hair we moulted over the bog, of the toenails we tore off with our fingers and left lying on the mat for months. We were ashamed of the cigarettes dangling from our mouths when we dozed off in the armchair, our nicotine-stained teeth and the smell of beer we exuded. We were ashamed of the sluts my grandmother met unannounced at breakfast and the way she always had to ask them what their names were. We were ashamed of our drunken singing, our filthy language, our vomit and the ever more frequent visitations of police and bailiffs. We were ashamed, but we didn't do anything about it.

It was three weeks before Auntie Rosie's husband, Uncle Robert, appeared at our door asking, 'Is Rosie here?' and we said, 'Rosie? No, is Rosie supposed to be here?' and he just broad-shouldered his way into the house, dragged Auntie Rosie out by the hair and kicked her into his car. And my sobbing cousin got into the back seat and disappeared out of my life until the next funeral. We were going to destroy Uncle Robert, there was no doubt of that, preferably extremely slowly and with a knife, and we swore that the next one to hear that he had cancer would take this honourable task upon himself. Because cancer lay in wait for all of us – Our Supreme Drinker had shown the way with style, and we were all agreed that making the age of sixty was the ultimate sign of a petit bourgeois. But if we were honest, we had to admit to relief that my Auntie Rosie and my cousin, Sylvie, were finally out of the house – their presence had been a little too confronting.

A miserable existence doesn't need to be complicated. Sylvie saw my father and uncles appear at the breakfast table in the afternoon where, after ritually smoking their first cigarettes, they would dig into the mince and tinned sardines to dispel the hangover from the night before. The greasy oil the sardines had been floating in would run down their chins until they wiped it off on the sleeve of an unravelling jumper, if they could find the energy. Then they disappeared from the house until returning drunk many hours later. Some people might call it a spiral; we saw it as a cycle. To avoid her father, Sylvie stayed away from school for the whole three weeks, watching me study and write my apathetic lines on the grimy kitchen table. Meanwhile she read books that made her smarter and more eloquent and would eventually open an even bigger rift between her and the rest of the family. In bed I could feel what she was thinking as she lay beside me wide awake and staring at the ceiling while listening to the snoring issuing from my father, who was sleeping it off with his mouth agape and his stinking socks still on his feet. Either that or she'd listen to Uncle Girder grind his teeth. How could she feel anything but disgust for our clothes, which lay in a pile on the floor waiting for my grandmother to throw them in the wash? I don't know what she found worse, the brown butts in the ashtray next to the bed, the sweat patches on the sheets, or my father's socks. She didn't say a word. I would have preferred her to call me to account for our lifestyle, taking me aside for a cousin-to-cousin talk. She didn't say a word and looked down on us.

'Kid, can't you take our Sylvie out for a walk sometime? The girl's gone all wan sitting inside the whole time.'

Where was I supposed to take her? She wouldn't talk to me and she'd looked at me with contempt when I'd used the end of my biro to scrape a lump of earwax out of my skull. Maybe they used cotton buds in Brussels, but so what? If you asked me, she could have shown a little gratitude for the hospitality. Anyway, there was nothing in our town to entertain a spoilt brat like her. She could have basked in the attention my friends would have given her in between hotting up their stolen mopeds, but Auntie Rosie would not have been amused. My friends were perverts and although lending them my cousin would have given me grounds to blackmail them with, I was just a little too honourable. The moment I stepped out of the door with this taciturn and haughty girl, I would be proud of her, I would look out for her. People had better think twice before risking a snide remark about her priggish little ways. But what was I supposed to do with her? Go for a walk? So that, while strolling along, we could ask each other what we hoped to achieve in life? What kind of hobbies we had? How school was going?

Taking Sylvie to the pub was my father's suggestion and it did not meet with the approval of Auntie Rosie. But she too could see that her daughter's complexion was growing more and more cadaverous.

'Which pub you going to?' she demanded.

'The Nook,' he replied. 'Or the Social. Whatever.'

'Will André be there?'

'How am I supposed to know if André's going to be there? You seen me with a crystal ball lately?'

'You'll be careful? And not too late?'

'What do you say, Sylvie? Would you like to go out with Uncle Pierre for a change?'

It annoyed me that we all suddenly tried to talk respectable the moment we spoke to the girl. I did it too. There was something about the look of her that brought it out in you.

Sylvie nodded and put on her coat. Our Kid – that was me – was going too.

'Rosie, lass, why don't you come with us? I know a few who'll be glad to see you. It'll do you good, a bit of fresh air.'

But Auntie Rosie didn't feel like it. 'What about you, Girder? You coming out for a beer?'

'Isaac Newton!' said Girder.

'What?'

'Isaac fucking Newton, I tell you.'

Girder was lying back with his feet up, watching a quiz show.

'*I'm sorry to disabuse you, Mrs Peters, but the correct answer to this question is Isaac Newton.*'

'Holy moly, you're not as daft as you look.'

'It's a repeat, dimwit. Hang on, I'm coming too.'

We had no particular reason for choosing the Nook that night; the pubs in our town were interchangeable. The chairs and tables were cheap and plain because they would only get smashed during arguments that started with something everyone forgot about immediately and were over again before the combatants had time to sober up. All the pubs had a jukebox with records that invariably brought tears to our eyes, even though no one would dream of playing them anywhere else. Roy Orbison was the greatest musician of all time: not just of the past and the present, but of the future as well, a future that could not possibly have anything good in store for us. There was nothing more beautiful than to sob into your last beer while the landlady swept the broken glass into her dustpan and the jukebox played Roy Orbison. And then to beg the landlady for one more beer, the last one, really the last one, and then we'd go home and leave her in peace to close her doors, which we would be the first to open again the next day. The difference between the pubs was a matter of very minor details, and the choice between them was most often determined by the number of outstanding tabs we had with some of the landlords, who we didn't dare face until we'd scrimped and saved enough to settle our drinking debts. Of the lot of us, my father was the only one with a regular job – at the post office – but he too could be in the red with the breweries by up to a few weeks' wages.

The Nook was run by a woman who had borne twin dwarfs, whose father disappeared soon after their birth and hadn't been heard of since. A woman alone with two identical, deformed daughters and deep in debt after pouring so much money into her pub. People drank enough, that income at least was secure. And when the dwarfs had to go to school and began making serious inroads into the money, she provided herself with a little extra by the means women always have at their disposal. Unfortunately, this seriously tarnished the reputation of her pub and wives began making unpleasant scenes whenever their husbands came staggering back from the Nook. The twins grew up in the bar. They played with their dolls under the pool table, set up a shop selling beer mats and plastic fruit on the pinball machine and hocked their toys to their mother's kind-hearted customers. They adopted the rough language of the men who spent their nights there, and by the age of ten they were filthy-mouthed slags with an endless repertoire of dirty jokes they recited to the amusement of all. By the age of twelve – they had already stopped growing – they had an alcohol problem because of their habit of drinking the dregs out of the glasses, initially to relieve their mother of the washing up.

In those days there was a popular pub called the Goat in a neighbouring village. The landlord owned an old billy goat and – for a hefty fee and to the great delight of the clientele, who almost died laughing – he would fetch it in from the stable and feed it extra strong beer until it was so pissed it stumbled and knocked over chairs trying to get back to its soft straw to sleep it off. It's quite plausible that this is what inspired the landlady of the Nook, but either way, at some stage, the two dwarfs began trying to drink each other under the table, and phenomenal amounts were bet on which one would stay upright the longest.

Long before we took Sylvie to the Nook, the twin dwarfs had discovered that, since their birth, they had suffered from a disease with a difficult name they found impossible to remember, and that it was extremely unlikely that either of them would make it past the age of twenty. Totally imbalanced by this tight deadline and determined to make up for lost time, they began boozing even more than before. On several occasions they had been known to leap completely shit-faced onto one of the many sticky tables, where they would lift their skirts for a grateful audience that stared goggle-eyed at their dwarf cunts with a mixture of disgust and fascination. I wondered whether it was my duty to prepare Sylvie for such scenes. Because something was definitely going to be dished up for our entertainment. There were certainties in our lives, that was our sole luxury.

When we stepped in through the door, the atmosphere was dull and familiar. You could stake your life that the blokes at the bar had been rambling on the whole time about disgruntled wives, divorce and alimony, subjects that were as usual here as the weather anywhere else. Two men were playing pool, but without any ambition to actually win; at the card table four old geezers were carefully studying the fate they were holding in their trembling hands; and the rest of those present were patiently drinking themselves down to the level where it gets hard to tell the difference between happiness and unhappiness.

'The first round's on me!'

These were the words with which my father always entered a pub. The dwarfs wrote down the order and passed it to their mother, who was busy letting our Girder knead her backside by way of hello. I saw the doubtful look on Sylvie's face as she watched her own flesh and blood grope the landlady and, at long last, a little red appeared on her cheeks. She was drinking lemonade lite. 'Sugar-free', she called it. As I was already in training to become the kind of man who props up the bar of pubs like the Nook, my father ordered me a diesel, the name we give to a mixture of beer and Coke. He thought I was still a little young for straight beer, but a boy my age who only drank soft drinks would have been too much of a disappointment.

'I see you've brought a nice piece of fluff with you, lads – but if the cops find out how old she is, there'll be hell to pay.'

That was André, and he was looking at Sylvie with disproportionate interest.

'It's family, André. This piece of fluff is our Sylvie.'

'Sylvie? You don't mean your Rosie's daughter?'

'The same.'

'Christ, that's a good-looking kid!' And André slid off his bar stool to shake my cousin's hand, which he did with exceptional courtesy. He kissed the back of her hand, gave her a captivating smile that laid bare his black, crumbling teeth, and then turned to me. 'Dimmy, lad, I feel sorry for you. It must be fucking difficult for you to keep your hands off your cousin.' His breath was foul, but that was no surprise, and I had steeled myself against the putrid fumes wafting out of his mouth. People laughed. Despite the inanity of the remark, I felt that they were expecting me to provide André with an answer. I kept silent and drained my diesel.

'Ah, lad, in our younger days we all pawed our cousins now and then.' And when I still didn't respond, he added, 'You're right not to speak.' And then it was time for the next round. Auntie Rosie was the unavoidable second topic of discussion. Everyone had heard that she had been spotted back in Arsendegem and now that we were sitting here with her daughter it was hard to believe the rumours weren't true. The other customers grilled us for details, but we kept our lips sealed. We listened with some enjoyment to the various theories, each wackier than the next, but all of them showing clearly that the mere

13

fact of Auntie Rosie's having returned to Arsendegem had been enough to blow life into feelings that had been given up for dead in our town. Since they weren't getting a sensible word out of us on the issue, all attention returned to Sylvie, with André announcing every other minute that she was a good-looking kid and a budding goddess, while everyone else searched her perfect face for features she had inherited from her mother. What surprised me was that being the centre of attention for all these coarse men didn't seem to make her uncomfortable. On the contrary, she seemed to feel a natural sympathy for them and kept laughing at every remark made by an increasingly drunken André, who had begun drinking and buying rounds at a pace that eventually only my father and uncles could match.

'Let me show you how I shit these days!' André announced to Sylvie in particular, pulling up a tatty shirt to display a hairy, lumpy, scar-covered torso. His intestines were riddled with cancer and to relieve himself he had a shit bag, which he had discovered one day to his great astonishment after waking up on an operating table. He'd never have to sit on a toilet again; it all just percolated straight into the bag dangling off his beer gut. 'Look!' And we looked. We watched the shit dribble into the bag. Sluggishly, as if the muck was in a tube somewhere deep inside and someone had just put his foot on it. Wet, sloppy shit with froth on top. My cousin stared at the brown ooze in André's shit bag as if she had a front-row seat at a demonstration of an engrossing scientific experiment. And her interest was only fitting, because the number was being performed just for her. Everyone knew that André wouldn't last until the next annual fair and we all admired the ease with which he hawked up his gobs and spat them in the face of death. He would die in style, partying up to his death rattle.

'That's it,' he said, 'my shitting days are done. Now I just need to flush.' He poured a full glass of beer down his throat. 'You have no idea how much I save a month on toilet paper.' It was gallows humour that tickled Sylvie, and she rewarded it richly with a flash of white teeth, the like of which we had never seen around here before.

'Drinks all round!'

Much has been written and plenty has been said about the character of dwarfs and it's a debate I'd rather stay out of, but that night the behaviour of the Nook's diminutive twins went beyond rude. They couldn't cope with a complete stranger reaping all the attention and being praised for her preternatural beauty. Of course, things aren't distributed fairly in life: they were monstrous and destined to die young. No one gets to choose their body. My cousin couldn't do anything about that. But the dwarfs were enraged with jealousy and lashed out below the belt by pointing out to everyone that the girly with the cute face might be laughing at our jokes and acting like she liked us, but in her heart she despised us. If you looked into her eyes you could see the way she looked down on us. You only had to look at her top and wonder how much it cost. Or hadn't we noticed that she was guzzling tight-arsed lemonade, lemonade bloody lite of all things, sugar bloody free? Could anything be more asocial and stand-offish? This good-looking kid – and this was so obvious you could smell it – was trying hard to put herself above her own family and doing everything in her power *not* to be a Verhulst.

You don't smack dwarfs, we knew that all too well – no one in our town would have raised a finger to those girls, not even our Girder. But this time they were abusing our ethical code and our hands started itching. We might sometimes beat the shit out of each other, but when it came down to it, Verhulsts stood up for Verhulsts. Always. Everywhere.

An unpleasant silence fell and everyone in the pub knew that it was up to my cousin to do something. To prove that she was one of us, that she belonged to our clan, that she embraced our customs, that she was part of the tribe. And that she wasn't here for a cheap, voyeuristic thrill, because if there was one thing we didn't like around here, it was peeping Toms.

And that made our entire table a target. Those pygmies were playing on Sylvie's family honour, knowing full well that it was true that she had hardly anything to do with us. What's more, my cousin bore her father's name, so strictly speaking she wasn't a Verhulst at all.

'Uncle Pierre, can I have a beer?'

My father would probably have found it easier if Sylvie had asked our Girder. The burden was on his shoulders and, at the same time, he was the one who had promised Auntie Rosie to deliver her daughter back home in an orderly state.

'Don't let them get to you, Sylvie, just ignore them.'

But that wasn't an answer to her question – she had asked if she could have a beer.

She got her beer. The first of her life. She didn't have a clue what the piss-coloured substance could possibly taste like, but given the stench in our bedroom, her expectations couldn't have been all that high. She straightened her back, assumed a theatrical and provocative pose with one hand on her hip (something she'd copied from my father – he always drank standing with one hand on his hip because that made it easier for him to throw his head back and open his throat), and drained the glass in one go. When she put the glass back down on the table with a manly bang – copied this time from our Girder – there were big fat tears in her eyes and the twist of her mouth made her look like she'd just gobbled down a whole bag of lemon drops. After the first sip of beer almost no one can believe that they will one day consume gallons of the stuff and I am almost certain that Sylvie was suddenly convinced that we were complete lunatics for pouring such vast quantities of filth down our throats every day.

André was over the moon, his night was already made, but Sylvie felt that she had been challenged and had evidently decided to accept that challenge in its entirety, because she immediately said, 'Give me another one!' No one touched a drop of Coke or lemonade for the rest of the night. Sylvie didn't and neither did I. The twins were bad losers and huffed off to their room, where they undoubtedly couldn't sleep a wink. André decided to turn my cousin into 'the real thing' and taught her some of the songs we used to sing. Some of them were fifteen verses long and I now wonder whether there's anyone left who can remember a complete verse. They were crammed with the filthy words that filled our ABC right up to Z, and the sight of my seriously underage cousin standing drunk on the pool table singing songs that were full of sexual innuendo, and doing it in a dialect that didn't suit her at all, filled us with such simple joy that we immediately got in another round to celebrate. And we all sang all the verses of every perverted song André struck up.

That night too came to an end. During the long walk home I supported my cousin, and my father and Uncle Girder supported each other. We kept on singing because we couldn't accept that yet another party was in the past, and we swore at the wives and mothers who hung out of bedroom windows to ask us if we knew what time it was. Behind us we left a trail of barking dogs and skittled rubbish bins. And urine, skilfully directed into a flower tub by our Girder. In Arsendegem there was zero chance of a conifer surviving for more than two years on an access route to a good pub because all our men would piss on it. Conifers don't like that.

'I have to do a wee too.'

We never did wees. We pissed.

'Sylvie, lass, can't you hold on till we're home again?'

She had to go. It wasn't that we were worried about her having to lower her jeans on the street – this late at night, anyone who would even comment on something like that had been asleep for hours. The problem was that Sylvie had lost all control over her body and had been hanging off my shoulder like a sack of sand for at least the last mile. She fell over the moment she stood on her own two feet, so we would have to help her if we didn't want her to get her shoes and legs wet. My father swore; Uncle Girder couldn't stop laughing and staggered back against the front of a house.

'Just fucking look at us at work here! The Verhulst family hits the town.'

'Kid, help your cousin now, lad!'

She was able to pull her own jeans down; she just needed some help with the button. I gripped her firmly under the arms while she squatted, letting me take her full weight. While we listened with relief to the splashing and splattering on the cobblestones, I thought about André's farewell from my cousin. He had asked permission to give her a kiss – on the cheek – and she had consented. Being allowed to meet her had been a gift from heaven – he'd had a fabulous evening with her and he told her that he would now die in peace. It was the booze talking, but beautifully.

Sylvie fell asleep in midstream; it seemed like the flow would never stop, and my father started getting nervous thinking about how he was going to explain the terrible state her daughter was in to Auntie Rosie. The closer we got to home, the quieter we became. We were almost there, but the prospect didn't cheer us.

Auntie Rosie was waiting in her dressing gown, with puffy red eyes.

'Where the fuck you been? Didn't it occur to you I'd be back here worried sick?'

19

We were sorry. We were sorry about everything. Our whole lives. That was us.

'And you, Sylvie, you must be proud of yourself as well and all.'

'The age of wonders lives on yet,' said Sylvie.

'What?'

'The age of wonders lives on yet, the weather's dry and my cherry's wet.'

That was from one of the dirtiest songs she had learnt that night, the then extremely popular 'Cherry Picker's Song', twelve verses long. And Auntie Rosie was so shocked that her hand shot out and left its print on the cheek of her well-brought-up daughter, who was too sloshed to burst into tears. Our Girder carried her upstairs and put her to bed, clothes and all.

'Come on now, Rosie, why hit the poor girl? What's wrong with the "Cherry Picker's Song"? She learnt the first five verses off André.'

'André? Did you see André?'

We didn't say a word.

'Did Sylvie see André? Did she talk to him?'

We didn't say a word.

'I asked you a question!'

We definitely didn't say a word.

'Does she know André's her father?'

'No!'

'Are you sure?'

'Rosie, of course we're sure. Sylvie doesn't have the slightest suspicion that André's her father, and if we told her she probably wouldn't believe us.'

'Dimitri, if you ever let what you just heard slip to our Sylvie, I'll scratch your eyes out. D'you hear me?'

'Yes, Auntie Rosie.'

We were all filled with pity later when Uncle Robert booted his wife into the car and sat his so-called daughter down on the back seat. But we didn't believe in poking our noses into other people's domestics and we left things to take their course, with our hands itching. The next funeral at which I would see my distant cousin again would be my father's. Five fathoms and a Friday.

The Drowned Baby Pond

Palmier was perfect mermaid material: she was slim and stank of fish. Her age was something we could only guess at, but if a clerk from the town hall had appeared to tell us that she had rounded the cape of a hundred years, we would have accepted it instantly. The odd person here and there remembered her husband, a farmer who had apparently adopted the behaviour of his animals. The children who were the product of this beastliness kept well away. Considering how old these children must have been by now, it was also quite possible that they had already died or been locked away in homes where they soiled their nappies to attract the attention of a nurse or protest against the imposed choice of television programme.

The gruesome story about Palmier that did the rounds in our town was, however, that she had given birth more often than could be ascertained from the official records and had drowned several of her newborns in her pond, the very pond in which some of us, including me in the company of my only-slightly-older uncle, Girder, liked to swim and where we used to laze naked on the pontoon and appraise each other tirelessly.

More than anything we were lazy, like all young people who need their energy to grow and develop Adam's apples and muscles and breasts and stray hair. Wendy with the corkscrew curls had them first, breasts, and her glorious backstroke left a magnificent twin wake in the water. She was already the proud girlfriend of my Uncle Girder, a girlfriend he had filched with ease from simple-minded, hyper-Catholic Werner, and when she was sunbathing on her back we would take our time to study those breasts – as small as they were – and their growth. After all, someone who looks closely enough can even see the progress of the little hand of the clock.

Most beautiful, though, was Helene when she had just climbed up out of the water and was lying down on the warm wooden boards of the pontoon. But maybe that applied to all wet bodies shining in the sun. I think that there, at Palmier's pond, we most recalled pictures of an idyllic tropical paradise or the advertisements for shower gel that undoubtedly inspired us. We enjoyed doing something that seemed so inappropriate. Youngsters frolicking naked: that was something for Africa or the Amazon, but definitely not this neglected backwater. By flouting geography, we cooked up a youth romantics might describe as untouched, simmering the days to make a stock for later reverie in the old folks' home. And if we weren't reminding ourselves of distant impossible worlds, we were calling to mind pictures (for colouring in, perhaps) of Greek youths, Spartans, ephebi ... And the girls too must have thought of those pictures as they watched us boys grappling in the water or tangled together on the pontoon in a seemingly eternal wrestling match. And who hasn't ever wanted to think about themselves in Olympic terms? The privilege of being an Olympian, if just for a moment. But Helene *was* one, her name gave it away. She had been suckled by the gods, her charms would be the making of her, she had the world at her feet.

There were always seven of us at the pond, a Christian number. Four boys, three girls, hot day after hot day on the water, wading and waiting for the fall that would put an end to the innocence with which we stood together along the side of the pontoon, seeing who could pee the furthest. Günther, a budding poet with red hair, always postponed his pissing so long that he was in an agony of spasms before triumphing with relief as he spouted an impressive victory arch clear to the other side of the pond. He was the invincible pisser until a bladder infection obliged a change of tactics and reduced him to mediocre performances. In winter he kept fit by pissing lines of blank verse into week-old snow. The girls preferred to pee in the water, laughing at the hundreds of tiny fish that gathered around their water-treading legs to gulp up the nutrients a jet of urine apparently contained. And so we learnt how to catch our fish on long summer days, diving under the girls' legs, waiting for them to pee and grabbing the gulping fish with our hands so that we could roast them later over the barrel we'd swiped somewhere along the way. I would never be able to smell a roasted fish without thinking back to those simple days; I realized that even then. After consuming the fish we lay on our backs on the warm wooden boards like emperors, like cats. It didn't matter if we got stiffies that, like sunflowers, stretched up to the sun – or was it Saturn in our heroic imagination? It didn't matter that the girls sneaked glances at us, comparing us

24

with the same innocence with which we had peeped at them.

Anyone who has ever lain patiently in the grass to watch a flower burst out of its bud or seen a butterfly hang up its cocoon casing to start life as a true avatar will understand the cosmic astonishment I felt on seeing Helene's breasts arise. A feeling you'd like to, if possible, preserve in jars. For later. A thimbleful on the tongue whenever life got difficult. (How many of those jars would I have already needed? Would I have any left?) I, yes, I was the first to see them. Whenever I've related this story in later life I've seen people thinking that it's impossible, that something so gradual is invisible. But believe me, a breast arises suddenly. With a 'pop' – but you'd need canine ears to hear it. She was lying on the pontoon the way she always did and I was looking at her. Not that perverted ogling, that came later. My eyes were just resting on her innocently. And suddenly there they were. It wasn't much, but unmistakably more than the elevation boys have on that part of their body. I had caught two small, unsuspected moles out in the process of throwing up their molehills. We all crept closer to Helene and spent the afternoon watching the modest Beginning of All Things. Every dawn that followed meant less to me. But when we heard that this was probably the place where Palmier had drowned her unwanted children and that we had spent the whole summer swimming in water that was mixed with the juices from the cadavers of the babies lying on the bottom, we never returned to the pond.

Palmier's livestock were gone, all she had left was a few horses and a dog. The horses were old and neglected and served primarily as a lawnmower for her land. Neighbours threw them chunks of bread now and then and sometimes they came up to the rusty barbed wire to be gently stroked by children who might grow up to work in the slaughterhouse, one thing didn't exclude the other. These horses would no longer supply tasty cuts, they were too broken down for that, and once Palmier died her elderly animals would, at the most, be sold for an organic song to a smart butcher who would grind them up to make inferior sausages. Palmier no longer bothered about her animals, just as she no longer bothered about herself. Her scrawniness and fishy smell were more than enough proof of that. Every aspect of her behaviour showed that she wanted to die and she obviously had our sympathy, but Palmier wasn't allowed to die and that made things difficult. Her land would fall into the hands of ruthless estate agents who would subdivide her entire property and sell it as lots for tasteless bungalows. We had already noticed the ostentation of the newcomers who had bought up the sites on the second-to-last property on Kerkveld Road: they erected gaudy letterboxes with stone cherubs in their front gardens and gave their brick bunkers names, casting them in iron so they could hang them on the front wall. If we wanted to avoid having the whole place buried in concrete, we had to do everything we could to keep Palmier alive. Of course, she would die, her expectations in this regard were no different from anyone else's, but every day of reprieve worked in our favour.

It was Grandmother Maria who gave us the task of cheering Palmier up by visiting her a few times a week and chatting about the weather.

Conversations about inane subjects perk people up. To extend her pointless longevity, we warmed up our leftover stew, a stew people nowadays might call an 'energy booster', and from which countless globs of fat looked up like so many eyes, as if Argus had been liquefied.

'Hi, Palmier, we've brought you something to eat. Terrible weather, isn't it?'

'Yes, young 'uns. Terrible bad weather.'

It hadn't been this nice and warm for months, but terrible weather rolled off the tongue easier and in the end we weren't completely wrong: the heat made Palmier stink even worse than she had in the winter.

Were we even born the last time she changed her underwear?

She immediately dipped her fingers into the stew, grabbed the marrowbones that were invariably present to optimize the flavour and compensate for the overabundance of sprouts, and sucked out the marrow. No surprise there, we all did that, but after polishing off the stew, Palmier also used a marrowbone as a straw to slurp up any leftover liquid. This made a frightening rattling sound that had us constantly wondering whether it was coming from the marrowbone or out of Palmier's withered lungs themselves.

'Kid, you up to asking her?'

'No. You?'

We were all too scared to ask, even though we had accepted and carried out many bigger, much riskier dares and seldom turned down an opportunity to prove our courage. We were all too scared to ask

Palmier if what people said about her in the pubs was true, that she had drowned a few of her babies in her pond.

What could the old bag do to us? Give us a beating? She hardly left her chair, perhaps because the weight of the shit in her pants made standing up difficult. She hardly had the strength to lift her soup spoon, so that it was sometimes necessary for us to shovel the food into her. What could she do to us? She could swear at us as much as she liked, that wouldn't hurt us, we were, in a manner of speaking, used to it, it made us feel at home. But still, nobody asked her the question. Not me and, surprisingly, not Girder either, even though he was already sixteen and almost a fully fledged gangster. We held our tongues and listened to the rumbling in her windpipe and her canary's daily singing exercises. That creature too saw its confines constantly shrinking, as Palmier hadn't mucked out its cage for centuries and the caked crap piled up ever higher. The canary was called Dicky, short for Dicky Bird, and he had adapted wonderfully to his situation, becoming a dedicated carnivore and feeding himself on the spiders that had wound their cobwebs around his bars, providing a bed for the thick layer of dust that filtered the sunlight.

Our fear of Palmier undoubtedly dated from our earliest childhood, when our parents threatened to lock us up in Palmier's yard when we were naughty. Because Palmier was a witch, that was why she wore a scarf over her head. It was why she was skin and bones, and why she stank. We no longer believed in witches, but some of our dread had lingered and our terror of Palmier had, in any case, been transferred to her watchdog. Our knees now shook at the sight of Blondi, a bitch that had a score to settle with us and would do so the moment she succeeded in breaking free of her chain. A dog's memory, after all, is a thing that should not be underestimated: like elephants and snakes, these quadrupeds have a lifelong capacity for recognizing their enemies and will not rest until blood vengeance has been exacted. Whenever Girder and I stepped into the yard the dog jerked her chain tight and we, suddenly realizing that it might be advantageous to believe in God after all, prayed that the concrete post the chain was anchored to might hold. The animal bared her fangs, which were rotten and must have already caused her insufferable pain, but whose bluntness would not save us from an agonizing death. On the contrary. A young and shining set of fangs would end our death throes so much sooner; our prospects were worse with teeth that were rotten. Our attempts to placate the beast by tossing a lump of mince at her feet didn't help – she kept barking until we had disappeared again and the last trace of our scent had been erased by Palmier's stench.

Blondi was old and decrepit, but lacked the typical canine intuition that everyone always talks about. If it was true that dogs have a sixth sense at their disposal, Blondi would have realized that no one loved dogs like we did. Not cats – they were reincarnations of stuck-up twats, who wore their fur as if they were draped in mink and spent their days whoring and flirting. They were unfaithful sluts. But dogs, we loved. Deeply. Including Blondi, definitely. A poor bitch without a pedigree, the pathetic descendant of industrious workers, who were probably masters of the arts of ratting and shepherding. She was spotted like a dog in a children's drawing, without any kind of gradation, and had short but sturdy legs and a snout that respected the primary laws of aerodynamics. Old age had left a thick membrane over her eyes, like the skin on fresh milk, and because of a combination of itch and boredom she had started to eat herself up. So it seemed. She'd bitten her legs to pieces, masses of flies had come to shit in the open wounds, and because of her attempts to break free, the collar with which she was attached to the chain had cut into her coat. Pus seeped out of her arse. Her function as a watchdog was limited to barking, as she was never let off the chain to attack anyone. Often the presence of a dog will bring out the best in a person and we couldn't understand how Palmier could calmly watch the suffering of her enslaved animal. We begged her to at least let Blondi off the chain. We offered to take her out for an hour's walk every day, on a lead if necessary, and even suggested taking her off her hands: buying the poor creature so we could provide her with a seemly dotage. Palmier wouldn't hear of it. Blondi was going to stay on that chain. The plan of secretly liberating Blondi one night got no further than a shiver of excitement at the thought of actually carrying it out. Our fear of Palmier was crippling. And so we kept bringing her stew with marrowbones and looked pityingly at her dog while she scoffed the food.

Cats have nine lives, but a dog dies every day. The chained, powerless and ancient bitch drew a steady stream of males that had been rejected by younger and much more attractive mates. These dogs were filthy, wretched pariahs themselves – that has to be said – mongrels that scavenged a living from the contents of garbage bags. They were mangy or limping, and had virtually no outlet for their urges apart from the legs of lonely children who took strays for playmates, only to be left behind in a state of confusion with muck on their trouser legs. Blondi was too old to offer any resistance. She stared into the distance while the universally rejected dogs took her hard from behind. Ramming her.

'That's it, kid,' said Girder.

'What?'

'Shagging! Screwing!'

That was in case I was wondering what they were doing.

And meanwhile we sat on our chairs next to stinking Palmier with all three of us looking at the misery of a stray having to make do with a totally burnt-out bitch with a suppurating hole, and Blondi on her chain, who was probably praying to St Francis of Assisi. Our awkwardness was crowned by the horrific fact that there was no mistaking the twinkle in Palmier's eye and the grin on her face, two things we never saw otherwise.

Nature is cruel. There were plenty of signs that Blondi's body was completely clapped out and we hoped that her soul was gadding about elsewhere, that she'd already vacated her shell, but just as it must have surprised my grandmother to fall pregnant with our Girder at a more or less ripe old age, so we found Blondi one day with five puppies hanging off her large but listless teats.

'Get rid of them pups!' Palmier ordered.

'We'll take them home with us,' we suggested.

'Cobblers! Get rid of the pups! Kill 'em! Put 'em in a sack and drown 'em in the pond!'

It was true, the puppies would have to stay with their mother for a good six weeks at least, and at Blondi's age that would have been the death of her. But still.

'I can't do it,' I admitted to Girder.

'Do what Palmier's asked you to do, kid.'

'No. I can't. Anyway, she asked you too.'

'You're piss weak, you are.'

'Up yours!'

'Up yours first, you gutless wonder!'

Palmier watched closely as we shoved the puppies in a sack, made sure it was sufficiently weighted and checked the sailor's knot she'd asked us to tie it off with. It was when we got back from the pond that Blondi started barking at us and growling with suds on her tongue and froth in her mouth. She strained against the chain, eyes focused in utmost concentration on our throats and the lumps that were stuck in them in the very place where our Girder had already grown a solid, jutting Adam's apple. We had a sword of Damocles and it was a dog. And it was simple-minded, hyper-Catholic Werner, whose girlfriend Girder had filched, who started nibbling on the thread that attached this Damoclean sword to the heavens by one day announcing, 'Remember we were on about setting that dog free and we were all too scared? Well, believe it or not, last night I cut the poor bitch's chain. God knows where she is now.'

The Tour de France

God created the day and we dragged ourselves through it. When we still lived like characters in the songs of Big Bill Broonzy, Omer organized an assault on the world drinking record. Beer drinking, obviously. It was one of the many strokes of genius by which Omer managed to fill his pub, the Liars' Haven, over and over. There was a compelling grandeur to his ideas, and the fact that they often got him into trouble with the police could only confirm it. The events Omer came up with were so extreme that the memories of those who relate them today are always questioned and it is only now, when many of the main characters have been wiped from the face of the earth, that I realize that the peculiar name Omer chose for his pub had the significance of an oracle: we who tell the stories of what happened there must go through life as liars, fabulists, mythomaniacs. But that never occurred to us at the time, and we weren't the kind to ignore a pub's existence just because the landlord had given it an ugly name. What's more, we knew plenty of pubs with beautiful names: the Mistletoe, the Olympia, the Rio, the Blind Finch – that must be enough.

Memory is life's consoling death throe, a higher form of afterbirth. It's only when memory has dried up that death becomes absolute. We start to decompose when others stop dreaming about us, and when none of the witnesses are willing to run the risk of being written off as a liar, the stories from the Liars' Haven will share our fate and be forgotten, which amounts to the same as never having existed. Some people leave a skull and a handful of bones, like a solitary brachiosaurus x million years and a couple of hours ago. Good for them, but we can still only guess at how they filled their days. Maybe excavating archae-ologists will dig Omer's skull or teeth out of the ground a million years from now, *beatae memoriae*. It's possible. They'll give the skeleton a name and it will be a hell of a fluke if it turns out to be Omer. And then they'll stand it up in a glass case as John or George or who knows what, next to the much older Lucy (who was probably called some-thing else too, assuming they even had the custom of giving each other names in her day) to illustrate the foolish course of evolution. But without wanting to prematurely underestimate the scientists of the future, I don't think they will have technology at their disposal to find out whether the skeleton in question was ever the landlord of a pub or prone to crazy ideas. No one there will ever know that Omer once organized a promotional stunt in the form of a nude bike race. A section of the population seethed with rage, not because riding a bike naked was seen as an offence against morality, but because the race was being held in an out-of-the-way part of town near the cemetery. Surprisingly enough, the influence of the priest was still large enough to counterbalance the police's sympathy for the project, and in the end

34

the fourteen godless participants appeared at the starting line in their undies. A compromise, they called it. The separation of church and state was no thicker than a pair of underpants. My father thrilled the large crowd that had turned out for the event by coming in a well-deserved second, because he had a good pair of legs on him. The success of this initiative was understandable, but that didn't diminish it. Omer knew how to lure the mob to his establishment, and a year after his legendary bike race he started assembling a team that would come together on the foundations of his pub to shatter the world record for boozing. He needed twelve men – where he got the number from was anyone's guess – and no one was surprised when, soon after announcing his plans, he showed up at our door to beg for participants. We weren't surprised either – all our days were predictable, even if we were never ready for them. No, the surprise came from our side when none of us was willing to go along with Omer's bloated plan. You could put us on bicycles naked and ask us to ride as many laps as you liked, we wouldn't shirk our responsibility when it came to entertainment – bring on the suggestions, we were up for it – but drinking as a sport was a bridge too far. Admittedly, my Uncle Heavy did sign up initially, even though he wasn't our best drinker, far from it, but he'd crossed his name off the list of participants at the request of a girl who presented him with a classic dilemma: it was her or the beer. My father wouldn't be talked round, he wasn't doing it, end of story. Our Girder was still underage and, to his deep disillusionment, excluded from participation, and our Herman fobbed Omer off with words that were simple but clear to all: 'Omer, I'm no loony.'

Of course, life went on, that's what makes life so difficult sometimes. The list of participants adorned the bar of the Liars' Haven. Every day we popped in to see who'd been added, nominating themselves to risk their arm in an attempt to claim this illustrious world record. Everything was arranged in detail, a doctor would be present to help the heroes through the difficult moments that would no doubt arise, and a bailiff would observe the entire proceedings, certifying the results so that the champion could see his name appear in *The Guinness Book of Records*. It would just be a name and that name wouldn't mean a thing to anyone – sooner rather than later our names are just an amalgam of dead letters, an anagram of the void – but someone who has been listed in *The Guinness Book of Records* has given a sign of life, proving that he has risen above the average, as enviable as that average may be. Mankind defined, that was *The Guinness Book of Records*, and someone who had done their little bit to push the limits of that definition was in a better position to fool themselves that they had been born for a reason. They could count themselves in one breath with whoever had swum the fastest, jumped the highest or sung the loudest. On a par with the creature with the longest tongue or the blackest cancer-addled lung. They were right there between man and monster as the *Homo erectus* who, in the ten-million-year history of swinishness, had drunk the heaviest. That was something to bring in the punters. We kept a vigilant eye on the growing number of participants, which had reached eleven by the eve of the event. Eleven brave lads, habitual drinkers thanks to boredom and tradition, marginalized from father to son. They threw themselves on a bar stool like a coat, but in this too they did not excel. The chance of victory was considered minimal given the complete lack of Verhulsts on the list, and what's more they still had to find a twelfth man with less than twenty-four hours to go. But we were not going to take part, oh no, anyone but us.

The world was saved in a moment of weakness. When we slipped into Omer's on the morning of The Great Day to stock up on cigarettes, we saw that he had finally completed his team. More from a sense of responsibility than from ambition, our Herman had relented and signed up as the twelfth and last man, and when this news spread to the rest of Arsendegem as well, the belief in a memorable evening that would score us a champion began to grow and ticket sales took off. When we saw a lorry delivering the rented folding chairs, we tasted what it was like to have an expectation and felt the tension as we watched the council workers build the stage on which our gladiators would battle the booze, a formidable adversary in anyone's book. On the stage were twelve stools, each accompanied by a wooden barrel into which the record contenders could spew at will. And hopefully they would, that was what people were coming to see. What's more, vomiting wasn't against the rules: the puked-up beer would not be deducted from the total and every swallowed pint would appear on the scoreboard. But they had to be swallowed first, in their entirety, and the bailiff's task was to differentiate between the swallowed drop and the drop that was spat out before disappearing down the gullet.

We couldn't say we were behind Herman's decision, but he had made it and that was a heroic deed in itself. Someone had made a decision and he seemed to us to need our support more than ever. We fried chips for him, we whisked eggs, we spread dripping on his bread, and regardless of whether his liver could cope with our schnitzels, we made sure he scoffed himself silly in order to line his stomach with a protective layer, what we called *a basis*. If the big shot wanted to be a sportsman, he had to learn how to live with being in top condition. What's more, he had the family honour to defend. Participating was more important than losing. None of us had asked him to participate, but now that he was, he had to bear the consequences. After his copious meal, we put him to bed to build up his reserves, and just before the competition was due to start, we sat him on the bog so that he could purge himself of the poisons from previous binges. Details that could make all the difference, even if Herman himself was less than convinced. When my father and uncles finally escorted him to the scene of the battle, none of us knew whether our Herman was mentally prepared to become *someone*, whether he was ready to return as a winner. Because that was how it was going to be: he couldn't lose, the competition was too weak and too thin. Fame was in his fucking pocket, and he hadn't even needed to study or play football to get it there.

It was autumn, but we were on a bender the whole year round and stories about lives like ours generally ignore the seasons. Still, death seems less of a trespasser when the leaves are pushing off from the trees and all of nature is dying coquettishly in one big artistic display. That night, I too heard the trees flapping their crowns like cheerleaders. The wind had travelled far and brought us nothing but thoughts that were too dark. It was the time just after slaughtering, when the cows know they have been pardoned for another winter so they can go on heat again and the melancholics among them bellow like sirens, grieving for the calves that have gone to cutlets. That was why the blue light of the police car cast such a beautiful glow on our bedroom wallpaper that night, because it was part of the divine choreography.

The doorbell rang but Grandmother Maria didn't budge from the bed she had just warmed up to body temperature. She had stopped answering the call of the doorbell at night because she knew it would be one of her sons who was so beer addled he'd lost his motor control and was downstairs fumbling for his keys. He'd be standing there groping in the immeasurable depths of his pockets, seeking a path between lighters, coins and bent cigarettes so that, if he was very lucky, he might fish out the house keys half an hour later. After which he faced the psychomotor test of getting the key in the keyhole.

The doorbell rang a second time and I heard my grandmother roll over again in the next room with a resounding curse, for which she would ask forgiveness at Lourdes the following summer.

I got up, looked out of the window and saw a policeman impatiently jiggling his legs. He looked like he was dying for a piss.

'Nan,' I called.

'What is it, kid?'

'There's someone at the door!'

39

'That's your father. He probably can't get his key in the hole again. Leave him to it. A night in the fresh air won't do him any harm.'

'It's the cops, Nan.'

'Again?'

My grandmother had stopped getting up at night for the police too. In the last few years she'd got sick of having to interrupt her sleep for friendly police officers who'd picked my plastered father up out of the gutter to deliver him home. There were times when the Arsendegem police corps most resembled a taxi company, and more than once they gave my father a lift to the front door only to show up again three hours later to drop off Uncle Heavy. It started getting out of hand when they helped our Herman up to his room and out of his tattered clothes. Ultimately they were providing a service to the whole town, because leaving someone out on the street to sober up could only cause accidents. In that sense we understood the constabulary's maternal instincts, but they had no right to exaggerate – we too had our pride. At other times they arrived to tell us that our Girder had once again battered someone during a drunken argument somewhere or other and was obliged, for administrative reasons, to spend the night in the cell, where he, in a manner of speaking, kept a spare set of pyjamas. The police always informed us so that we wouldn't be worried when he didn't show up for breakfast. As if we were bothered when our men didn't come home for a few days. When they were in top form and wanted to get drunk at all cost, we might not see them for a whole week. What's more, we didn't even eat breakfast, at least not until we'd smoked half a pack of cigarettes.

But when a policeman adopts the bad habits of a vacuum-cleaner salesman and rings the doorbell up to five times or keeps his finger on the button until someone finally opens up, one can suspect something serious.

When my grandmother finally opened the door, the policeman didn't seem at all happy to have found someone home.

'Good evening, ma'am, sorry to disturb you this late at night, but are you the mother of Herman Verhulst?'

'That depends.'

Everyone around here knew the Verhulsts, the police best of all. Apparently this youngster was new to the force and had been sent to us as his baptism of fire.

'May I come in for a moment?'

'Hang on a sec. I'm standing here in me dressing gown with no teeth in. I'm hardly fit to receive visitors. What d'you want?'

'It's rather serious, I'm afraid. Are you sure I can't come in for a moment? It's not easy to tell you this at the door.'

'Kid, get me teeth from upstairs so I can give this gentleman a respectable welcome!'

There was some lukewarm coffee left in the pot and the policeman accepted it gratefully, not expecting the bitter taste of our chicory. If we hadn't put the bag of sugar down next to his cup his face would have dropped right off. As soon as Nan had her teeth in, she let him resume talking.

'Before I go on, ma'am, you're not a heart patient, are you?'

'Is this any time of night to be bothering people with questions about their heart?'

'I have to ask, ma'am, I'm sorry.'

'What's it about? I want to go back to bed.'

'Your son, ma'am, Herman Verhulst . . .'

'Yeah? What's he up to now?'

'. . . is currently in a comatose state.'

'Look, officer, I'm an old woman on a pension that's not nearly enough. At fourteen I was working in the weaving mills of Aalst and Dendermonde. We started at five and I rode me bike to work, rain, hail or shine. Every second I spent in the toilet got docked from me pay. At seventeen I fell pregnant with a baby boy who was so big they had to cut us open to get him out. In the end I gave birth to ten children, nine of them alive, and I've spent me whole life washing and cleaning up after 'em. In other words, I didn't go to no university. I know that all me sons, including our Herman, come home nights in a terrible state. You should have seen the state our Pierre was in yesterday. But I don't know what it's called. *Comatose* or whatever it was you said. Although, I can kind of imagine it, a *comatose* state. That's an everyday event round here. I've seen it all. But maybe you can get down off your high horse and talk like a human being.'

'Comatose is a scientific term, Mrs Verhulst. It means that you're not quite dead, but not really alive any more either.'

'That's what I was trying to tell you, officer. You see that here every day of the week. Maybe I'm comatose too, if you put it like

42

that. Is that possible, d'you think?'

The policeman assumed an expression as if to say that he was a policeman and not a doctor.

'If our Herman was dead, you'd have said so, and not that he's in a comatose state or any other kind of state, you daft bugger. *Comatose*, come off it. Is that Latin or what?'

The policeman shrugged. By this stage he was undoubtedly cursing the police chief who had sent him off with the job all his fellow officers hated. This task always fell to the rookies; the old hands applied their experience to stamping official documents and writing parking tickets.

'Look, officer, I'd like to take me teeth back out now and go back to bed. And if you'd be so kind, don't bother us with bollocks like this again. It's four o'clock in the bloody morning. Comatose state, my foot. Scientific term, my arse. The stuff you have to listen to in a life-time.'

Three weeks later our Herman came home with tape on his face and skin that exuded the penetrating reek of hospital. He was held together by an impressive number of stitches and the plaster on his left leg had been signed by all the nurses. Magnificent nurses, according to Herman, and he'd promised them a bunch of flowers each because they'd stuck to his bed for three whole days whispering sweet noth-ings into his ear, which was something they apparently did with all the coma patients, as the only way to bring back their urge to live. And see, our Herman had awoken from his coma and would shortly

43

be cheered as a hero. Because he had become a world champion, that went without saying. After adding eight pints to the previous world record for beer drinking, he had manfully climbed into his car, even though he could hardly stand. The whole dumbstruck pub had watched as our Herman miraculously managed to open the car door and insert the key in the ignition. And when he also started the car and drove down the street in a reasonably straight line, everyone was convinced that they had stood face to face with one of the most remarkable drinkers of all time, someone whose world title could not in any way be put down to coincidence. Just a few minutes later our Herman was already on the motorway, albeit on the wrong side of the road and for no more than a few seconds. The impact must have been terrible.

Despite the superhuman amounts of alcohol in his blood and despite his grievous traffic offence – all things considered, enough to take away his licence for life – his insurance company didn't hold him liable at all and paid every last penny of his hospital and garage bills. Typically for our Herman, he'd had a head-on collision with a stolen car and as a bonus he was able to go to the town hall a month later to receive a medal for writing off a gang of hoodlums the police had been chasing for months. He himself was thrown through the windscreen to the music of Roy Orbison, which he'd been playing at top volume during his suicide drive, and he resolved that he would have a son and call him Roy, in gratitude for the miracle of life. We advised him against it.

Our world champion pisshead! Herman Verhulst! His father would have been proud of him! And we prepared ourselves mentally for a whole life of answering the question as to whether we were related to that particular Verhulst, Herman, every time we spelled our name for the clerk of the court.

The only one who couldn't bring himself to show any enthusiasm was Girder. As a minor who had been excluded from the competition, he felt discriminated against and he was convinced that he and he alone deserved the title. What's more, he questioned the validity of a competition that improperly narrowed the concept of boozing. First, the contestant could just happen to be having a good day, the kind of day when you knock back beer after beer without going belly up. Those days do happen, days of grace. And second, the drinking session was limited to the watery lager produced by the De Geest brewery, whose wort left a film of stench and doom over our town. Girder had expected more from a world championship; he'd hoped that it would reveal the total pisshead to the world, someone who had mastered the full range of the boozer's repertoire. Any fool could neck himself into oblivion. The art was to neck yourself into oblivion and do it again the next day, and the day after that, and the day after that, until you were the only man standing. With the contestants boozing for weeks on end if necessary. And they shouldn't be allowed to limit themselves to beer. Vodka and whisky and cocktails and all kinds of gruesome distillations had to be covered as well. Girder's goal was the incorporation of all these basic principles in an attractive form, a competitive structure, as it were, and he arrived at the solution with a speed none of us thought possible. Because our Girder had discovered that his ideas about the total souse coincided with the ideas that Géo Lefèvre had had about the total cyclist. Lefèvre, designer of the very first Tour de France, had aimed for a race that was so tough that only one contestant would reach the finishing line. Our Girder's test of strength would be like that too, and he immediately began to develop the concept with a dedication he had never raised for anything before.

Scissors and glue reappeared in the life of the almost-adult Girder. In the shed he stuck the map of France (scale: one to one million) to a large sheet of cardboard, to the great relief of his mother, who saw her son converted to arts and crafts, something that would eventually stimulate him to learn a trade and keep out of pubs. He then traced the whole course, made up of 19 magnificent stages, on the map. Start and finish in Paris. After some calculations, he decided that five kilometres on the map were equal to one standard glass of alcohol, which clearly meant that even a reasonably short stage of 180 kilometres would involve drinking 36 standard glasses of alcohol. Against the clock. But our Girder was, after all, looking for the most complete boozer, an exceptional talent who could only be discovered by setting the bar at an insane height. Healthy transparent piss, that was what the contestants would be passing for the nineteen days of the race.

Extending the analogy to the bike race further, he came up with three classifications, three jerseys to earn. The yellow jersey was for the leader and final winner, the person who completed the course in the

46

fastest time. The green jersey was for the explosive sprinter: the neck-it king. And the polka-dot jersey could be captured in the mountains, where you proceeded by guzzling strong drinks like whisky and vodka.

The plastic racing cyclists I had once played with – in my dreams they had been Lucien van Impe or, more often, Bernard Hinault – which were also the only toys I hadn't been able to get rid of and had wanted to keep because of a feeling that manifested itself even then as an incomprehensible nostalgia, those miniature racing cyclists suddenly disappeared into Girder's pockets to serve as tokens on the board. The competitors would be allowed to advance their cyclist one square per drink. A bit like snakes and ladders, but for pigs.

Our Herman thought the whole idea ridiculous, if not childish, and refused to participate. Of course, he'd already grabbed the official title and had a reputation to lose; we guessed he thought it wiser to rest on his laurels. My father was known as a big drinker, but was limited in his capacities: red wine sent him straight to sleep. What's more, he'd already lost a third of his stomach to the nasty habit of mixing beer and wine and Campari and gin with anything else he could get his hands on. Since then he'd settled down and become your typical proletarian drinker, a beer man by necessity as much as choice. He was drinking himself to death, but preferred to do it discreetly, seeing it more as a social blessing than a sport. Our Heavy was down with a bout of gout, so Girder had to look for competition outside the family circle.

Unlike Omer, Girder quickly amassed a magnificent group of entrants, a total of eighteen enthusiastic boozers, among them a reasonable number of minors seeking revenge for their exclusion from Omer's competition. As a result the race could be seen as a clash of the generations or a battle of succession. What's more, someone from far outside the town had shown up, the president of a drinking club in the faded seaside resort of Ostend, a reputed swine with hardcore supporters in motorbike leathers. His body was a charnel field of tattooed skulls and he would definitely add a certain air to the competition. This was someone you'd have to watch in the Alps; whoever kept this ogre from claiming the polka-dot jersey would have something to put on their CV. Girder had not just opened his competition to the country as a whole, he also accepted women. Lardy Zulma from Restert Lane (a widow who showed her deeply humane sense of cosmic emptiness by throwing herself at gormless young men) was undoubtedly a contender for the final victory; her phenomenal reserves of fat, enough for a multitude of pre-war winters, would allow her to break down the alcohol in no time flat. We could already look forward to her mounting a marathon escape or taking on the Hell's Angel in a duel on the flanks of the Tourmalet. Of all the contestants, our Girder was the biggest outsider, the one who would have to do the most on willpower alone, making a sozzled return from the group of the dropped and launching a break when he was already legless.

Eighteen contestants: it was a success already, and our Girder felt giddy when he realized how easy it was going to be to make history. Because that was a certainty, it couldn't go any other way: this alcoholic parlour game was the best of its kind, no one had designed a better method to unveil the most talented piss artist to humanity. It was clear that soon, all over the world, people would be playing their own Tour de France. Based on the original by —. It was only logical. And something so pregnant with history demanded epic words that would eternally commemorate our Girder as the pioneer of heroic drinking. What we lacked was a newspaper of our own, a paean, a megalomaniac eruption, a boozed-up bard drawing his inspiration from the almost delirious journalists who, from the very beginning in 1903, applauded the glory of the bicycle version of the Tour de France. Something like:

'Today, through an imaginary France, our professional boozers display their degenerate but immense energy. From Paris to the blue waves of the Mediterranean, from watery lager to pastis, from Marseilles to Bordeaux, from distilled vinegar to lukewarm wine. While passing through these sun-drowsed, pink and dreamy towns, cutting across the fields of the Vendée, up the entire length of the slow and stately Loire, these men and women let the fluids cascade down their throats, frenzied, inexhaustible, knowing that along the way they will encounter all kinds of momentary blackouts and rising nausea they will have to shake off. Withstanding headaches and diarrhoea, they will tap new energy, calling on their ambition to become something, even if only by the grace of a strong stomach and good liver function, which is still, after all, better by far than being absolutely nothing. Over many hundreds of miles, converted into many gallons of killing booze, ranging from whisky to cognac, under the biting sun and nights that shroud them, they will encounter purposelessness, idleness

49

and laziness, numbed and unwilling gullets, recalcitrant gag reflexes. In the titanic struggle they have taken upon themselves there will be moments of stupor. At times they will not be ashamed to let their sphincters go, to turn pale of face, to jabber and lose their heads. Because the bodies of these men and women will be wrecked on this most difficult of all routes through this imaginary France, but the wreck will become legend, which cannot be said of the many who are whole yet senseless, whose deaths will be neither more nor less than the convergence of themselves and their ancient meaninglessness.'

The person who was visibly overjoyed in this period was Grandmother Maria. She had noticed an inexplicable enthusiasm in her youngest son, predestined for the scrapheap though he was. Every school he had ever attended had expelled him after a cursory period on probation. Work was something he didn't do, and on the very rare occasions he did, compelled by an abject shortage of cash, he would end up bashing his employer as an expression of the general dissatisfaction that just happens to find a better outlet with one person than another. And now, out of the blue, he was coming home with bike-racing jerseys and diving into the shed to saw up topographical maps on thick cardboard. Her youngest had taken up cycling, and to judge from the fire in his eyes, he was going to take that cycling so seriously that he would soon trade drink and cigarettes in for a life dominated by healthy sport. The Lord had tormented her, letting her mumble many a prayer that He might guide her youngest to the straight and narrow, but He had done it. And thanks for that.

The entire race would be ridden in a caravan in the garden of Jowanneke's parental home. It was the caravan Jowanneke's father had converted to a painter's studio to keep himself occupied, and in which he had strung himself up so as to never be occupied again. The map of France and the toy racing cyclists lay in the middle of the plywood-lined space, flanked by a scoreboard, a stopwatch and a fridge to keep the drinks cold. Puke buckets were not provided: the garden was big enough and Jowanneke's mother would be away in Benidorm on a beach holiday until at least the last stage.

At midday on an arbitrary second of July, Girder bundled his three jerseys under one arm and rode off on a stolen but sadly rusted ladies' bike to the start of his first ride in the Tour de France. The prologue. A short time trial over three beers, nothing to worry about. Necking beer was a question of technique, you just needed to master the knack of opening the back of your throat. And our Girder had. So doing it three times in a row couldn't be a problem. An extended sprint was right up his street and nobody was surprised when the prologue finished with him in the yellow jersey. It was still too early to draw any conclusions; he knew that better than anyone. The differences were less than a second. But even so. The gleam was still visible in his eye when he appeared at the table that evening in his yellow jersey (mince with tomato and onion), and it was clear that it was going to hurt when he had to surrender that jersey to someone else. To Lardy Zulma maybe: she ran like a diesel and didn't start getting thirsty until she'd downed a whole bucket.

Our Herman thought Girder looked ridiculous perched at the table like that in a yellow jersey, but that had nothing to do with his sense of aesthetics.

'So, Eddy Merckx, I see you rode well today. No doping, I hope? Have you had to piss in a pot yet?'

'You're just jealous. Too gutless to join in, and now you've got a big mouth. You'd already be an hour behind by now anyway.'

'Herman, leave our Girder alone. He's turning into a real rider. You'd do well to take up a sport too, 'stead of giving all your money to the landlady of the Nook.'

'Yes, Mum. I'm sure you're right, Mum.'

'Don't take it to heart, son. It does us a world of good to see you racing. Really, it does.'

'Thanks, Mum. I love you too.'

The seriousness of the race became apparent when our Girder went to bed early that evening, anxious to be fresh in the morning. Tomorrow the first test awaited – riding from Amiens to Chartres, 195 kilometres or 39 glasses. It wouldn't lay the power relationships bare, the stage was too flat for that, but you'd immediately feel whether you were up to that kind of distance, and even this early in the race, letting yourself fall too far behind would not be a good idea. There were only two negligible climbs, each to be surmounted by drinking one Trappist beer: alcohol content, ten per cent. The first rider to down their Trappist beers would start the day after tomorrow in the polka-dot jersey, the only jersey with balls, but Girder was doubtful about becoming overly ambitious in that area. The green jersey suited him better. He was a Freddy Maertens kind of rider. There was a sprint after twenty lagers, and another after the twenty-seventh. They were the ones he had to win. And beyond that: make sure he finished. Because that, obviously, was the rule: anyone who failed to completely finish the stage didn't need to show up the next day.

The starting shot was fired at ten in the morning, the hour at which our postmen were already falling off their bicycles. And the competition unfolded like a real bike race. At the start of the stage everyone chatted cheerfully while drinking a glass in the ever-thickening mist of cigarette smoke, realizing that there was a long way to go and taking cover in the pack. Eighteen people, crammed together in the caravan. After ten lagers, which hadn't split the pack at all, the competitors began walking back and forth between the caravan and the orchard to piss. Twenty-nine glasses to go: you'd have to be mad to start a solo run for the finishing line from here. The first tragedy in the history of the Tour de France (*Girder Version*) occurred at the fourteenth glass. Wilfried, though born into a pro-German family and a beer drinker by both nature and philosophy, suddenly tumbled off his chair and had great difficulty climbing back up onto it. He took more than an hour over his next lager – with pitiful little sips, like a child learning to drink. And finally he was sensible enough to give up. There were just seventeen competitors left in the race and a little more room in the caravan. This relatively short, almost pancake-flat race would at least trip up the amateurs. How many stages would it take to find out who needed to take who into account? As Wilfried staggered home, the self-declared pretenders to the green jersey began eyeing each other. There was a handful of bonus points to be shared out between the five leaders after lager number twenty, but when did the sprint start? At which point did you start throwing them back? And how fast could you recover after that kind of effort? Would you pay the price fifteen kilometres later when the first climb loomed up before you?

Our Girder launched a smart breakaway on his eighteenth lager, grabbed the maximum at the first intermediate sprint and then, in a manner of speaking, started coasting. He was riding in virtual green, that was his target for now.

It would be fair to see this entire first section as a warm-up. It meant nothing compared with what was scheduled for the coming days, and yet the atmosphere had already grown drunker. Fits of laughter came one after the other, every now and then someone provided light relief by striking up a dirty song, and more and more often people stopped bothering to go all the way to the back of the garden, hauling out their tackle to piss on the wheels and plywood sides of the caravan instead. At least, with the exception of Lardy Zulma, who resolved that starting next stage she'd be bringing a piss-pot.

A crate of beer! How many people can say that – that they've drunk an entire crate of beer between two meals? It happens some-times, at a wedding or after a divorce. But you're sick for days on end. Here they'd downed their crates and the race hadn't even got going yet. At the first Trappist beer Kurt shot forward; he was the son of the brick-maker, another genetically determined souse. For a moment, glances passed back and forth in the peloton, but they let him go. He had the stage victory and a twenty-minute lead to go with it and he was totally shit-faced.

'The Idea . . .' wrote Dino Buzzati after a stage of the Giro d'Italia, with a very emphatic capital I. 'It is for the Idea alone that riders drive themselves into the ground, even if they have plenty of money. And it is the Idea and nothing else that draws the crowd to the roadsides. The crowd doesn't believe in money, it doesn't believe in special interests, it doesn't even believe in muscle. It is the Spirit, the crowd says, only the power of the Spirit that turns the wheels, climbs the Falzarego or the Pordoi and sets the records.'

Our Girder was shit-faced too . . . for the Idea. Thirty-nine glasses of alcohol, hell, you don't get that under your belt without noticing. But he had his green jersey draped over his shoulders, that was a real boost. As pale as a corpse and with a beard of dried vomit around his mouth, he sat down that evening at the table, where the smell of roast pork and cauliflower cheese was almost too much for him.

His mother was worried.

'You're overdoing it, son. That's no good neither. How far you ride today?'

'A hundred and ninety-five kilometres!'

'What? A hundred and ninety-five? Like I said, son, you're over-doing it! You've not done a whit of sport for years, and all of a sudden you've got the bug and right away you're tearing along for hours a day. You have to build up slowly, that's what I think. And all on that rusty old boneshaker of yours.'

The next day, when Girder came back half-conscious from the third stage, which he only lost on the last corner, he found a brand-new racing bike waiting for him. A gift from his mother to show him how much she appreciated his finally turning over a new leaf. Those things cost a fortune. We'd seen them in the window of the bike shop on School Street and the prices were a disgrace. Bike racing was supposed to be the national sport, but we would have never even dreamt of getting a racing bike. And now all of a sudden one was standing there. A blue Colnago with beautiful, curved handlebars, the horns of a rutting ram. A very serious derailleur. Click-in pedals. The very latest brakes. The seat padded with a special gel to avoid boils. We knew how small her pension was. We knew that we managed to drink up her small pension long before the end of the month. And we knew that to buy this bike she must have secretly pawned something, maybe the jewels she had inherited from her mother, who had died young. Jewels she was so attached to you'd think they were her mother herself. And it didn't stop at the bike.

'Look what else I got you!'

A water bottle. They'd thrown that in for free.

And at the sight of the water bottle, our Girder ran straight to the toilet. It had been a difficult stage after all.

Over three effervescent anti-nausea tablets, our Girder thought about his Tour. A stage win should be possible, a couple even, and just before Paris there was another time trial, sixty kilometres this time; he'd have to win that. But first he had to get over those bloody mountains. He was most worried about the Hell's Angel. The guy was a sponge. He never got overly ambitious, he never rushed, he just drank calmly the whole time without showing any signs of drunkenness. At the end of each stage, he jumped on his motorbike and rode back to Ostend as coolly as if he'd just been to the shop to buy some organic vegetables. He seemed indifferent to all three jerseys, the carry-on about points left him cold, but it looked like he was going to ride up the Champs-Elysées as fit as a fiddle and quite likely all alone. If our Girder conquered the mountains he gave himself a chance of holding on to the green jersey and maybe even grabbing yellow. Lardy Zulma had never drunk whisky, not a drop in her entire boozed-up existence, not even in a chocolate; there was a good chance they'd drop her in the Pyrenees. Kurt had been impressive at the start but had already taken on a yellowish tinge thanks to his completely overburdened liver. He might be able to stretch it to the foot of the Alps, but after that he'd collapse if he tried to ride another inch. Although you could never be sure. Our Girder was okay with it, whisky. That's to say, he got it down his throat the way he got olives and dried figs down his throat – without a stroke of enthusiasm.

The zone of truth was approaching, the imaginary mountains were jagged on the horizon, the second- and third-category passes were ready and waiting for the spectacle. The ride to Mourenx, over the peaks of the Aubisque and the Tourmalet. A flat three-lager approach. Then a difficult zone of seven glasses of wine. White or red, drinker's choice. And then it started: a glass of tequila, a shot of mescal and half a bottle of whisky. In the descent, four glasses of water and half a glass of milk to keep them on their toes, and then uphill again, the other half of the bottle of whisky. All in all a short stage – no denying – but what a ride.

When the twelve remaining riders stepped into the caravan that morning, they realized that the diary lay open at a historic day. The whole garden stunk of piss and the bleach Jowanneke had used in a vain attempt to rid the caravan's wheels of the reek of puke. The same stench hung in the caravan too and nicotine had started to drip from the plastic ceiling. All the elements needed to write history were present in the correct proportions.

The Idea . . .

No one knew what possessed our Girder to shoot out of the starting blocks like a madman at ten o'clock that morning. Up till then he had paced every ride with intelligence. He *read* the race, as the experts say. But that morning he rode up the Aubisque like a snorting stallion while the other riders (let's stick to describing it in the terms of a real bike race) were still calmly peeling their bananas. Lured by the legend, enthused by the Idea. Or was he so disgusted by all that whisky that he couldn't wait to put it behind him? That same morning he had sold the magnificent racing bike to a shady scrap-metal merchant for a tidy price to pay for this enormous quantity of booze. Maybe it was old-fashioned Catholic guilt that now drove him to the summit of the Aubisque at a furious pace, realizing that returning home without a victory was now impossible. Disbelief floated in the eyes of all who saw it. It was superhuman. It was so superhuman, it was monstrous. This was the alcoholic interpretation of Eddy Merckx *and* Fausto Coppi *and* Jacques Anquetil *and* Odile Defraye *and* some horrific monster at the same time. He didn't even take the time to go outside to water the side of the caravan, pissing his pants to maintain the pace, diving down the mountainside and preparing to storm the Tourmalet. Girder unchained. In the peloton they didn't bother trying to launch a pursuit – no, they sipped their whisky calmly and wondered whether this Mephistophelean maniac would change up a gear in the last forty kilometres.

The Idea ...

We were home watching the coverage of the real Tour de France when the doorbell rang without a trace of menace. My grandmother had her teeth in, all of them, and that must have come as a relief to the policeman who saw her open the door.

'You again? If you've got any more questions about me heart – I've lived the last forty years with a pig's valve and I'm better off with that pig's valve than I ever was with the one God gave me. Come on, what's it about?'

'Good afternoon, ma'am. Are you the mother of Karel Verhulst?'

It was true, sometimes we forgot: our Girder's real name was Karel, but we'd been calling him by the nickname he'd picked up on a building site for so long that hardly anyone remembered. I didn't have an Uncle Karel. I had an Uncle Girder.

'Our Girder, you mean.'

'May I come in for a moment, Mrs Verhulst?'

'Just say it at the door, officer, I'm sure you'll manage. I just mopped the floor.'

The policeman no longer insisted – he was a fast learner.

'I'm afraid I have to inform you that your son has been taken to hospital in a highly critical condition.'

'You come here to tell us about one of me boys again? Don't you lot down the station have nothing better to do? Critical, you say? Critical? Be critical of your own kids, if you've got any! Our Karel has turned over a new leaf. He's off racing his bike right this moment.'

'I'm afraid, ma'am, that your son was taken in to hospital about an hour ago with delirium tremens.'

'There you go again with your Latin. It's always the same thing with you. If you're so keen on Latin, go visit the priest. He'll be glad to see you for once. Come back when you've learnt to talk like a human being because I can't be bothered listening to your drivel for another second.'

And she slammed the door.

Only the Lonely

We knew that the bailiff would subject all our furniture to his cool appraisal, and when his eye finally settled on our television set and stayed there, we could have given ourselves a kicking for being so stupid and not hiding it at the neighbours' or a friend's until we'd put the whole rigmarole of debts and threats behind us. Not our telly? Surely he wasn't going to confiscate our telly? Not today? He sipped the coffee we'd offered out of politeness and we noted the way his mouth twisted for want of sugar.

'It's the chicory, sir.'

'Beg your pardon?'

'In the coffee. I see that your face is about to drop off because it's so bitter. It's our mother. She always dumps a ton of chicory in the filter to stretch the coffee. She lived through the war. I'm sure you understand. She had to go without and now ...Would you like some milk in it?'

Friendliness, it was worth a try. Maybe we could save the telly by being friendly and offering the man some milk, even if we personally thought it an obscenity to drink coffee any way but bitter. Regrettably enough, we felt our chance of retaining the TV shrink considerably when the milk turned out to be off, and not just a little bit either. The stuff was already halfway to turning into something that most resembled East German butter. The bailiff spat it into his cup and for a moment we were worried he might vomit. Not that we felt sorry for him, it was his own fault. He was the one who'd carried off the fridge a month before to clear my father's unpaid tabs. It was good for a bailiff to realize what it was like to live in a house he'd visited.

This time we owed the bailiff's visit to my Uncle Heavy and his sudden, maniacal interest in playing fruit machines. Of course, he was right to realize it was easy to win money on one of those machines, easier than earning it by working for a boss. But that was balanced by the fact that it's much easier to lose money on that same machine, and probability was something our Heavy had never heard of. He was, in short, a little naïve to think that fruit machines were designed by altruists, and on top of that, he was unfortunate enough to get credit from the landlady of the Maritime. She had caught wind of his gambling fever, his weakness, and anyone who takes advantage of a weakness is, according to Darwinist scale models, an intelligent creature. The street our Heavy had gone down came to a dead end: he started gambling to pay off his gambling debts.

'You're not going to take our telly, are you?' asked Heavy, because it was up to him to take the initiative; we expected that much at least.

'I won't need to take this television if you can immediately pay your outstanding debts. Can you do that?'

No, he couldn't. Our Heavy was totally broke, his mother didn't even need to check his pockets for coins before throwing his trousers in the washing machine. And there was no question of his brothers or his mother advancing him the amount he had to cough up, not so much because they were afraid they'd never see it again, although that could have been a reason, but because they were all equally skint. My grandmother's pension had already been shared out completely between various breweries.

Our unfortunate furniture would no longer fetch a decent price at a public auction; too much frustration had been taken out on it. The chairs creaked, the armrests were gone, some of the legs had been glued back on. What did we have left for the bailiff? The wristwatch I'd been given for my first Holy Communion? The sign of the zodiac necklace I'd been given for my first Holy Communion? The camera I'd been given for my first Holy Communion? But even if people bid for all of those things it wouldn't cover a thousandth of Heavy's debts. The bailiff wasn't even curious about our record player as it was around that time that humanity had switched en masse to a belief in the inevitability of the CD player: rumours were rife that soon you wouldn't be able to buy a stylus anywhere. Since it was the same story with linen typewriter ribbons, he didn't touch our noisy Remington either, although it was still an excellent piece of equipment. Progress was doing fine without us. No, it came down to the TV or the washing machine. We could count ourselves lucky if they didn't get lugged out together.

'Does the television still work properly?' the bailiff asked. The disaster had taken its definitive form.

'You're not taking our TV?'

'Do you have another suggestion?'

'It's not even mine, it's our mum's.'

'Quite likely. But if you'd wanted us to keep our hands off your mother's possessions, you should have gone somewhere else to live. You are officially resident at this address, so this is where we have to come when you default. That's the law. And the law is the law.'

'Who says so? Who says the law's the law?'

The bailiff remained silent. That made it hard to outsmart him.

'Fine,' Heavy tried again, more diplomatic now, 'but can't you come and pick up the telly tomorrow? One day can't make that much difference.'

'Mr Verhulst, you have already had three extensions of payment and you have ignored the same number of orders to pay. You have already far exceeded the final date. We have to draw a line somewhere. All things considered, we have been very lenient. I'm sorry.'

'You're not at all sorry! If you were sorry you'd leave the telly where it is, end of story. One day's grace, is that really asking too much?'

'I don't see what difference an extra day would make.'

'Roy Orbison!'

'Excuse me?'

'Roy Orbison. On TV. Roy Orbison is on the telly tonight. His comeback. After all these years. Don't tell me you don't know Roy Orbison. "Ooby Dooby", "Running Scared", "Mean Woman Blues" . . . All his. Believe you me, sir, if you knew what Roy Orbison stands

64

for, you wouldn't hesitate. Leave the TV for one more night. Just one evening. Six hours is all we ask.'

We smelled a chance. A whiff of a chance.

My father, who had wisely stayed in the background so far but was a master in the art of timing his contribution, bounced up, sucked in a lungful of air and launched into the first verse of 'Only the Lonely'. Uncle Herman joined in on the second line. The Von Trapp family singers. 'Only the Lonely', mega-hit that it was, meant nothing to the bailiff, whose otherworldliness was not going to be remedied by my father's grotesque English. When singing along to English songs he generally limited himself to the vowels, admittedly always managing to get them in the right place.

Disaster plan number three consisted of our Heavy starting off about his mother.

'Just look at the old dear for five seconds, will you? An old woman. Her telly is all she's got left. Those German shows on Saturday evening. She looks forward to them all week. And that Australian series makes her forget her woes. You couldn't be so heartless as to take away a poor woman's only entertainment? Or would you have her watch the washing machine every night?'

Bailiffs were heartless, it was the primary recruitment criterion: a complete lack of flexibility.

'I don't like having to tell you this, sir, but to be a bailiff you'd have be a monumental cunt, otherwise you wouldn't be able to stand it. I'm sure your boss is very satisfied with you, congratulations.'

That was disaster plan number four. There wasn't a fifth and it wasn't necessary either. My grandmother emerged from the kitchen with a bucket and a rag, just the way a commemorative statue would represent her.

'Mum, what are you up to?'

'I can't let him take a filthy telly away with him, the glass is dripping with nicotine. What's he going to think of us?'

'That takes the cake. The sod plunders our home and you ...'

And so, bearing a respectable television, the bailiff bid us farewell – we wondered for how long.

The challenge now facing Heavy was to find a TV in less than five hours so we wouldn't miss a second of the resurrection of Roy Orbison. Heavy's own preferences were more in the coloured direction. He loved black female singers with stunning legs and breasts that had been moulded to fit mechanics' hands. Tina Turner was the pinnacle, even if he admitted that she'd done her best work in the days when she was still getting regular beatings from her bloke. It was his brothers who worshipped Roy, putting him on such a lofty pedestal that I couldn't understand why he was virtually absent from the obligatory lists of musical highlights that appeared everywhere at the end of that strident century, their century. Elvis had hundreds of imitators, but Roy Orbison was inimitable. If you said he had the voice of an opera singer, it would be a compliment for the opera singer. Roy was Roy, no one came near his voice, end of discussion. What's more, we loved his tragedy. Losing his wife, Claudette, in a motorbike accident and then, two years later, having to live with two of his three children being consumed by the fire that razed his house. A crap life, that's what it was. If humanity was divided into two groups, we would definitely fall into the same category as Roy Orbison. But what made the singer so irrevocably loved was that he wore his mourning with so much conviction that everyone forgave him when he remarried, hitching up with a German dirne this time. He wrapped himself in the blackest black, including sunglasses, and tolerated no other colour on his body. No one could catch the man out with a smile on his face. His career slumped and, inevitably, he wanted it that way. He knew The Hole that is dug for all of us. We accepted that yawning chasm, but Roy leapt into it. We interpreted his plummet as a longing for his departed lover. It must be wonderful to fall to the source of all your thoughts. But he rose again. Had he licked the elixir of life from Barbara's German lips? It was possible, and no one held it against him. Our Barbaras were yet to come. But Roy had risen and would tread the planks once more in the Cocoanut Grove, a club in LA.

When my father laid his timeline next to his idol's, he saw nothing but parallels. The singer's high points matched *his* peaks, and the two of them had tumbled simultaneously into life's cellars. According to the logic of a loser, the fact that Roy was now more or less rising from his own death could only mean one thing: my father too had reached a turning point. In its symbolic value, this evening easily matched the consolation of the great metaphors. Since the rumour of Roy's return had done the rounds, we had spoken of the Cocoanut Grove as if we'd been regulars there for years. It was a place of myth, a dream to share.

Every day the Cocoanut Grove popped up in our stories, relevant to whatever we were talking about at the time, and that evening on TV we would finally see proof that Roy Orbison was singing his definitive turnaround. And his change of direction was our change of direction, the themes of our lives were bound up together; we believed in the representation of thoughts as a series of cogwheels: one thought turned and set another moving. Our Heavy better make sure he got his hands on a telly.

Publicans sometimes set theirs up on the pool table, but reserved this, thank God, for the rare occasions when TV was a social event: a cycling classic, a football final. A performance by Roy Orbison could have been a social event – after all, you could still find some of his most moving slow numbers in jukeboxes, and as long as those singles earned money they'd stay there – but his era was about to end. Younger drinkers were under the spell of a different kind of music. None of the publicans wanted to insult our taste in music, but they didn't want to drive away the other patrons either, they had to think of their turnover. We understood that. When things were explained politely, we understood them.

Come six o'clock, our Heavy still hadn't laid claim to a TV and Roy Orbison would be starting his set at nine o'clock sharp. Roy Orbison didn't keep his audience waiting. That kind of pretentiousness was reserved for artists who *thought* they were great. There was no question of our watching at the neighbours'; our reputation was a greater barrier than the wall between us. We could have watched on the unmanned sets of friends who were spending the evening in the pub, but birds of a feather flock together and it takes one to know one, so they realized that leaving us alone in a strange home was not the safest course of action. In families where women ruled the roost and the remote control, the evening would be given over to romantic biscuit-tin films, and we rejected once-only special offers to programme a video just for us because a live show was not made to be watched afterwards – that would rob it of its magic.

The eighth, ninth and tenth hours weren't listed in our dictionary, so it was no surprise that it was the eleventh when Heavy put an end to his brothers' gloom by informing them that he had found a TV.

'I don't see any TV. Where's the TV?'

'There's some people we can visit. We can watch it there.'

'Who?'

'No one I know. Does it matter?'

'You mean you knocked on a complete stranger's door to ask if we could maybe watch their telly? For fuck's sake! You should be ashamed of yourself. Now we're cadging company. How low can we sink?'

'Guys, you think I'm doing it for my own entertainment? You want to see Roy Orbison, fine, you get to see Roy Orbison. Ungrateful bastards.'

Entering strange houses empty-handed was not customary, not even for us, but what did you give to people you didn't know when you didn't have anything to give? Well, there was one crate of beer left in the shed – that would have to do. And for the missus we took the aspidistra that had stood on the TV. Simultaneously solving the problem of finding a new place to put the aspidistra.

The arrangement our Heavy had made for us was in the first row of houses you saw driving into Arsendegem from the west. Holes. Rat traps. The kind of dumps we would have been living in if my grandmother hadn't taken us in. Number 84 stood out because of the satellite dish on the roof, proof that there was never anything on TV. But tonight there was: Roy Orbison. Live at the Cocoanut Grove. And we were going to experience it here. In the rat traps of Arsendegem.

To be honest the man who opened the door was not the kind of person we'd expected in a house like this. Dressed in a good suit, he had gleaming black hair and a magnificent moustache he obviously pruned daily. And his skin was brown. Not *brown* brown, but brown. Say, somewhere between yellow and brown. The kind of brown your face would turn if you spent the whole night leaning over an ashtray full of smouldering butts. That brown. Whatever. Later, looking back, our Girder said it was the brown of a grown man's dick.

'Welcome!' said the man.

We understood what the word meant – 'Welcome!' – but used by itself like that, we only knew it from books and films. We were sure about the films, at least. We'd never actually said it to anyone else and we'd never heard anyone say it. Not in real life. Maybe that meant we'd never really been welcome anywhere before now.

'My name is Sawash!'

'Sah-what?'

'Sawash.'

'Sawash? Wash? As in car wash?'

'Yes, as in car wash, ha-ha. And this is my wife, Mehti.'

'Pleased to meet you.'

My father shook hands with our host and hostess and his brothers followed suit. So these were foreigners. There'd been a lot of talk about them lately. We did have a couple of Spaniards in town, old Communists my father had ideological debates with down the pub, but you couldn't call *them* foreigners. This was a different category.

'We are from Iran.'

'Iran? Really? Iran on TV just yesterday.'

Iran was on TV every day. But where exactly it was, we didn't know. The only problem we had now was communicating. These people had only just learnt the basics, but in a sense they already spoke our language better than we did. Their Dutch was proper. It was *Dutch* Dutch. Now we'd have to drop our Flemish accents and limit ourselves to a few simple words per sentence.

'You fan Roy Orbison?' Herman asked.

'No. Is he from Belgium?'

'No. Roy Orbison American singer. Texican singer, in fact. Big hit "Only the Lonely". Wife dead in crash. Bang! Children dead in fire. Boom. Whoosh! Get it? Now Roy sing again. On telly soon. Nine o'clock. You turn on then, thank you?'

We looked around. Lying on the table were dictionaries, English and Belgian newspapers, and books of poetry.

'You educated man? Read poetry no less.'

'I learn poems by heart to absorb the rhythm of Dutch.'

'Absorb rhythm?'

His wife had to smile. Mecca melted.

'You tell us poem, Mr Sawash?'

He didn't feel like it, that was clear, but his integration was at stake. He looked at his wife, his wife looked at him. Then she said, 'I shall recite one. One verse.' She had come to the rescue of her husband. A woman like that could only be from abroad.

She coughed, scratched and began. 'Underwater all the empty bottles are full . . . The silence there stays soundless . . . Like a fortress behind plate glass . . . Like a violet dried in a dictionary.'

We applauded wildly. Our Girder stuck his fingers in his mouth and whistled. And we basked in the blush that took charge of her cheeks. That was something else we'd found out: brown people blush too.

'That very beautiful,' said Herman. 'You read good. Beautiful. Beautiful. Me touched deep inside. You read at my funeral, please.'

'"Underwater all the empty bottles are full." How do they come up with something like that?' My father would think back on that sentence often.

Maybe it was time for us to hand over our gifts, but my father just stayed sitting there in the armchair with the crate of beer between his feet.

'Um, we bring beer. We not come with hands empty. You allowed drink beer from religion?' He was still finishing the sentence when glasses appeared on the table.

'You no make glasses dirty. We drink from bottle. Is real Belgian, very typical, drink from bottle.'

We toasted. Iran. Belgium. And Roy Orbison who, in ten minutes, would mark the return of happiness with the beat of a gong. Then we presented the lady of the house with the aspidistra. True, we should have done it the other way round, but what the hell. Mehti accepted it gratefully, repeated the word aspidistra several times – making us realize that it wasn't such an ugly word after all – and added that they were glad to finally have Belgian visitors. It wasn't easy establishing contact with people.

'Just come to pub. You make contact straightaway. The Social. You sign up pool club. I teach you play pool and drink. You friends straightaway.'

'What time is it?' my dad asked. He knew what time it was, but would have found it impolite to simply tell them to hurry up and turn on the TV.

'Even without you, nine will strike,' Sawash said.

'What?'

'It is a line of poetry I have learned by heart. I think it beautiful.'

'I'll stick to those full bottles.'

The show had already started, but the stage was still empty. The camera zoomed in on the restless audience, sometimes locking on a single face for so long that it must have been somebody famous. But we didn't know them and neither did Sawash. The people were sitting at small tables covered with champagne buckets, but we were having a good time too, with our crate of beer. Behind the curtains, guitars were being tuned, the moment was approaching.

'Do you mind if it's a bit louder?' asked Girder, and without waiting for an answer, he turned the TV up to maximum volume.

'The neighbours!' Mehti said. Actually, she had to shout it.

'You tell neighbours Girder best friend. Neighbours sure to know Girder. Tell neighbours they make trouble, Girder smack 'em in gob. Neighbours understand.'

That was that taken care of.

The band members appeared on stage and suddenly it was as if history had treated itself to a second and better chance, because Roy Orbison was being supported by none less than Elvis Presley's backing band. We didn't have anything against Elvis. Elvis was, well, what was he? Something big. No doubt of that. But Roy Orbison was bigger. Then came the violinists, dressed in black, and all wearing replicas of the famous sunglasses. Man, the atmosphere was electric.

'Is that Roy Orbison?' asked Mehti.

'You three bricks short? That's James Burton. Used to play guitar for Elvis.'

'Ah, Elvis. One for the money and two for the show.'

Typical. Elvis, she knew.

'The songs of Elvis Presley have been translated into Sumerian,' said Sawash in an attempt to burden us with pointless information. Surely they weren't going to go on about Elvis and desert languages? In a few seconds Roy Orbison was going to appear. The guest musicians stepped out into the footlights: Bruce Springsteen, Tom Waits, k.d. lang, Elvis Costello, Bonnie Raitt, Jackson Browne, Jennifer Warnes, you name it, a whole pack of them had shown up.

'Is that Roy Orbison perhaps?' Sawash this time.

'Of course not. That's not Roy Orbison, that's Bruce Springsteen. I'll tell you when Roy Orbison's there. Patience, Sawash, patience. All in good time.'

And that time had come. Roy stepped out onto the stage, tossed the strap of his guitar over his head and gave a firm but friendly nod to the audience. It really was him. They hadn't deceived us. Roy Orbison had truly arisen, hallelujah. We jumped up from the sofa, just like the audience on TV jumping up from their chairs, and gave him an overwhelming round of applause, equally convinced that he could hear it.

'Is that the custom here?' Sawash wanted to know, but it really was time for Sawash to shut up.

'So that's Roy Orbison!' Mehti said. 'An old man.'

The backing vocalists, led by k.d. lang, opened with the clearly masterful sentence 'Dum dum dum, dumdy-doowah', and Roy joined in with 'only the lonely'. We were in heaven. For years we had listened tirelessly to his records, but never before had we seen the man sing his epic songs. Now the time had come. And immediately we noticed that Roy hardly opened his mouth. At least not far enough for us to ascertain with certainty whether he had any teeth left. It was a miracle. He hauled octaves out of his voice box that would have had any other human being opening their mouth so wide it ripped at the corners, and he seemed to do it effortlessly. He just picked the high notes out of his nose. What's more, he didn't make a show of twisting his hips or swinging the microphone over his head like a lasso. None of that. He just stood there. Straight. Aware that he had already become a legend in his lifetime. And those clothes! A cowboy shirt with cord trim. On anyone else it would have looked ridiculous, but not on Roy Orbison. He humiliated the New Wave musicians who were shooting up like mushrooms at the time and drawing everyone's attention to their emptiness with their black clothes and Mardi Gras mascara. Roy Orbison gave black another dimension. He was a one-man New Wave and he played rock 'n' roll. We had to drink to that.

Finally we could show Mehti and Sawash the true face of Belgium by jumping on their sofa with wild delight and hurling the cushions at the ceiling while Girder danced on the table with his arms wrapped tenderly around a chair. The people they had taken for a grim, introspective nation were now pushing aside the furniture in their living room to dance. I saw that my father already had hold of a statuette and was walking it through the room. Our Herman had found himself an equally exemplary dance partner by taking a painting down off the wall.

'Hey, Mehti, don't they do belly dancing in Iran? Come on, Mehti, show us some belly dancing, we've never seen that in real life!' And before we'd had a chance to really think it through, we were standing there chanting, 'Get 'em off, Mehti! Get 'em off, Mehti!'

Yes, we could already feel it, the return of Roy Orbison had changed the direction of history. There was no way round it: we would have to prepare ourselves for a long period of intense happiness. The musicians on stage seemed to sense it too. Bruce Springsteen was beaming, and it wasn't because he was happy about being Bruce

Springsteen; no, being allowed to stand in as a backing musician for Roy Orbison had fulfilled his true childhood dream. You could tell that the other musicians felt the same way. Tom Waits jerked spastically over his keyboard. His head went down almost to his feet, and by the sound of it they must've turned the volume of his instrument right down because he kept hitting the wrong chords and couldn't even keep the beat. The only pain in the arse was Elvis Costello; we couldn't stand his ugly mug. Putting the most favourable twist on it, he could pass for an annoying economics student, and his pseudo-intellectual image left us cold. But otherwise we had no complaints. This was the kind of performance that only comes up two or three times a century. Without Elvis Costello it would have been once a century.

For eight numbers Mehti feared for the continued existence of her flowerpots, and then Roy launched into the masterpiece 'In Dreams', a song that tells the story of a love who is no longer there, nowhere, unless it's in our dreams, which doesn't make waking up any more enjoyable. That song was too much. At least for my father, who couldn't bear so much epic beauty. He buried his face in the cushions of the sofa and started blubbing. Our Herman explained it to our host family. 'P. sad. Let him be. P.'s wife gone. Long time now. Bye-bye. His wife go away with someone else. She whore. Understand? His wife fucky-fuck with other man.' And to make sure everyone understood, our Herman illustrated his words with simple yet unmistakable movements.

Mehti's attempt to console my father didn't help. In fact, the touch of a soft female hand on his shoulder only made it worse. Our Girder made a brief attempt to cheer him up ('You're not going to lie here blubbing all night just 'cause some other bugger's giving it to the dirty slut for a change?'), but it was a lost cause. After all, the next song was 'Crying', another enormous tearjerker. They left him lying there, my uncles, and went back to dancing on the table as 'Candyman' moved the performance back into a more cheerful, swinging mode. Meanwhile Sawash had sat himself down on the sofa on the other side of my father and was telling him that he knew what it meant to miss someone – he'd left his own mother behind in Iran – and for a second we were afraid we were going to have two of them sitting there snivelling.

My father was still crying when the show finished and he kept it up while we dragged him out of the door, thanking our friends the Iranians and begging forgiveness for the inconvenience. We promised that we would be back soon to pay for the vase we'd knocked over dancing and we meant it, no matter how much they insisted it wasn't necessary. But Roy Orbison had returned, happiness beckoned, the future was ours for the taking.

Dad's New Girlfriend

Our interest in the female body remained a constant, but the emphasis went through phases, like most things in life. The period of our fanatical ogling and rating of breasts persisted for a long time but finally gave way to the inevitable phase of the backside, an area where there were fundamental differences in our preferences, which left more room for debate. When a woman we'd never seen before appeared at the door asking for my father in a posh voice, we were at the zenith of a period in which we devoted great attention to the assessment and appreciation of women's inner thighs, in consequence of which we were doubly grateful that it was summer and the female in question was wearing a divinely short skirt.

Still, we came very close to missing this apparition altogether because immediately after the doorbell rang, Grandmother Maria said that it was probably the police again or the Jehovah's Witnesses.

It was our Girder who opened the door anyway and lowered his gaze to take in that skimpy piece of fabric, miniskirts, by the way, being the reason we liked to watch Italian films. His habit of whistling through his teeth whenever he saw a firm piece of flesh was already familiar to us.

'Well, love, if you're a Jehovah's Witness, you can convert me right now. Where do I sign up?'

'Is this where Pierre Verhulst lives?'

'Our P.? Are you after our P.? Come in!'

We were used to women appearing on our doorstep and didn't usually need to ask which of our men they had come for. We knew each other's types. Our Girder was especially attractive to slags who almost certainly derived a secret thrill from getting thumped by their bloke. Sluts on stilettos, they were usually drenched in body lotion that smelled like dog shampoo. They almost always smoked Marlboro Lights with tight little puffs they had once rehearsed in front of a mirror, and had sagging jawbones and noses that formed an angle of more than forty-five degrees. They varnished their nails mauve and had inauspicious names like Cindy, Wendy, Chantal or Nadine. They could cook spaghetti and had a reputation for knowing the alphabet. His conquests were often girls he'd picked up on the weekend at a disco called the Partridge and he brought a lot of them home with him. As Girder and I shared a bed, his was the type I got to know best in all its embarrassing detail.

Our Herman bagged a completely different kind of woman. With his innate melancholy and mournful features, he aroused their maternal instincts. The women who took him under their wing, very patiently at first, invariably believed that they would get him on the straight and well-lit path of virtue. Courageous. But brutally ugly. They had horsy teeth that could stand up to punches, bulging eyes, Habsburg chins and the kind of character that dirty bitches share with magpies. They had shrill voices and invariably thought they could look down on us just because they'd got close to a computer at some stage and managed to pick up an accountancy diploma along the way. Our Herman's tragedy was that he had married and impregnated all of his conquests – costing him a shedload of maintenance – and that all those harpies had gone to the courts later to stop him seeing his kids. We were quite capable of understanding that women might disapprove of our lifestyle, but they could at least have the decency to not marry us first.

I preferred to open the door for women who had come for our Heavy. Magnificent women I was secretly in love with. They had brains too, which was why they always dumped him after a while. They almost always had children with someone else and were using him as a springboard to a divorce or a new life. Black-haired or redheads, their smiles were unblemished by philosophy, and they came from all over Europe. One was called Vandenbroeck, the next Angelowsky, but they all had a certain class, so much so that I hoped they would put up with our family long enough for me to grow up and swipe them from my uncle, accepting the beating I would inevitably receive for doing so.

But the woman who was now standing at our door and asking for my father was a stunner. An educated stunner, because she was carrying a leather case and wearing glasses that were so trendy there must have been fetishists who collected them. Maybe she worked at a bank or a law firm. Whereas my father's taste in women was beyond disgusting, almost perverted, with a mild preference for tattered cleaning ladies and elderly, boozed-up barmaids. Since his divorce he had only shown himself in public with a girlfriend once, a monstrous tart, a substitute for my mother. I was ashamed of him, but the reactions of his inner circle were so extreme that after that he kept his amorous escapades to himself. In the end that was better for everyone, especially me. And now this wondrous thing was standing on our doorstep asking for him. You can understand our astonishment. Girder waved her in and grinned behind her back as Herman immediately tried to force a glimpse between her legs. The skirt was definitely short enough, deliverance had to be possible, and our hunger would probably be stilled as soon as this creature stopped dithering and sat herself down on a chair.

'Just sit down,' Girder said, 'I'll call our P. for you.'

'A crate of beer for the first to see her knickers,' Herman said quietly.

'Two crates,' replied Heavy.

'It's a deal, two crates.'

Our Girder's stomach had only just been pumped, but he still thought three was more like it.

It wasn't easy to find a chair for her. Most of our chairs were on the point of collapse and had been totally unreliable ever since my father had hurled them at the wall in a drunken fury. But we couldn't explain that now, she'd find out about that side of his character soon enough, that was a pleasure we couldn't deny her. Finally we got her to sit down at one corner of the coffee table, so that she had a table leg between her legs and had to spread them slightly to sit comfortably. We stayed where we were, in the kitchen, at a safe distance, appraising this figure who, we now realized, would have made an equally favourable impression if we had still been stuck in our breast obsession. We were no longer sitting, we were *lying* on our chairs, overwhelmed by the stakes of three crates of beer.

Although we weren't watching it at that moment, the TV was on. Our brand-spanking-new TV was on: in three years we'd have paid it off. Our TV was almost always on, the open hearth of the poor in spirit. BBC 2. Darts. Fat Brits with acne-scarred faces standing behind a line and trying to score *one hundred and eighty* with three darts. Watching it – or rather, not watching, but enduring it – was somehow Zen-like. The same with snooker, which we sometimes fell asleep to at three in the morning.

'Do you watch this often?' the lady asked.

At that moment, of course, we were watching something else – the female *one hundred and eighty*.

'As much as we can,' said Herman.

'To keep up our English,' Heavy said in an attempt to right the situation, and they burst out laughing, not stopping to think that by doing so they were revealing their most rotten teeth.

Meanwhile our Girder had come back from the bedroom. 'I can't wake him up! I'll try again in a few minutes.'

'I'll wait,' she said, 'I'm not in a hurry.'

It was hardly a newsflash, but my father hadn't been in bed for very long. We'd all heard him come home that morning. We'd heard him piss in the sink while drawing on the oeuvres of Nina Simone, Julio Iglesias and Roy Orbison. We had then heard him fall down the stairs, dragging picture frames off the wall as he went. Next up was a re-sounding curse, a string of magnificent swear words aimed at my mother and several Liberal politicians. After that he got drawn into a war with his shoelaces, and when he had finally, after many labours, removed the clothes that stunk of an entire tobacco plantation, he opened the street-side window and started, buck-naked, to loudly sing the *Internationale* in something he took for Russian. With his head pre-sumably spinning and full of loving thoughts about Marx and Lenin, he rolled into sleep. That must have been four and a bit hours ago.

'Would you like a coffee?'

She didn't want anything.

'Something else? Tea? Soft drink? A beer maybe? It's hot enough?'

Nothing at all.

'You're a cheap date, you are.'

Our Girder, in a whisper, to me: 'If that's going to be your new mother, lad, you're going to have a very hard time keeping your hands off her.' And he raised one buttock.

'Hey, Girder, you old goat, aim your farts at someone else.'

'I didn't fart at all, you drip.'

'No, really? What stinks, then?'

'Maybe the inside of your own rotten nose?'

. . . New mother? I hadn't looked at it that way. Was that a possibility: my father hooking up with someone else and us going to live
with her? Someone who dressed us, telling us that green socks really
were monstrous under red trousers? Someone who'd have my father
rushing straight home after the working day, who we'd go on holiday
with for two weeks to the Ardennes, where we'd stay in a chalet and
take snaps and rent a kayak and go for walks in bright plastic coats?
Would she enquire about my scholastic activities of an evening, maybe
even helping me with my homework so that I – who knows? who
knows? – might get acceptable marks after all and squander my
prospects of sloth and eternal unemployment? We would start to brush
our teeth again, deposit our underpants in the laundry basket instead
of leaving them lying around in our stench until a passing grandmother picked them up and used a pumice stone to scrub the skid
marks out of the pores of the cotton. We would start paying our bills,
mostly on time, and reach for a rag if we pissed on or past the toilet
seat. We'd pick our cigarette butts up off the carpet and put charcoal
insoles in our shoes.

'Maybe she'll let you take your baths with her.'

The woman sat there, feeling queasy from the looks we kept giving her
and uncomfortable with the table leg between her feet, which made
it even more difficult for her to relax. Of course, she saw us conniving
and speculating, and when that started to get through to us, we realized that things would be a lot pleasanter for her if we involved her in
our conversation. Our Herman took the lead and addressed her.

'Sorry, but is that table leg getting in your way too much?'

'I beg your pardon?'

'That table leg? Isn't it in the way?'

'Oh! That! No, not at all, thank you.'

'Oh, good, because it's really completely in the way for me.' (Bwah ha-ha-ha!)

Good intentions, that was as far as we ever went. But she didn't seem to have a sense of humour anyway – there was some room for improvement there. It was a sure bet we were straining this woman's nerves, and we were already amusing ourselves with thoughts of my father being called to account for his brothers' sleazy behaviour. Because his blood ran through our veins too, she'd know that as well as anyone, she must have attended a biology lesson or two in her time. And he'd have to bend over backwards, saying, 'But my brothers, love, well, they're just pigs. I'm not like them at all.'

'Are you Dimitri by any chance?' she asked suddenly, presumably from boredom.

'Me? Er, yeah.'

'I've heard a lot about you.'

The idea of my father telling a brand-new girlfriend about his son was enough to make you weep. You could only feel sorry for someone who was weighed down with offspring and had to inform every new woman that he had once been stupid enough to put a bun in a tart's oven, thus seeing his chances of a new relationship narrow to a hair's breadth because very few of those women were willing to take on someone else's kid.

'How old are you?'

'Me? Er . . .'

Thirteen. I was thirteen and lived with my father and my uncles and their old mother in Arsendegem, a town the great cartographers forgot, an ugly backwater, but a great place for drizzle and pigeon fancying.

Our Girder felt the conversation degenerating into a thing of little value – he was right – and made another attempt to wake up my father. That was, without a doubt, one of the most difficult tasks under the sun, and I was glad to see Girder taking it upon himself for once. As thirteen steps were too many to climb twice in such a short period of time, he now screamed from the bottom of the stairs, 'P., lad, get up, will you? There's a chick here to see you.'

'Huh?'

'I said, there's a chick here to see you.'

'A chick? What's her name?'

Our Girder, to the woman: 'What's your name?'

'Nelly Fockedey!'

'Yeah?'

Our Herman, fumbling under the table for his still-burning fag end: 'Fuck a day, all right. Yeah!'

Our Girder again: 'P., her name's Nelly Fuckaday.'

'Moron. Pull the other one. Let me sleep.'

'I'm serious, Nelly Fuckaday, she's been sitting here an hour and she hasn't even had a drink.'

'What's she look like?'

'Not bad. I reckon you could turn her into a nice earner.'

'That's no help. I asked you, what's she look like?'

'Brown hair. Bit over nine stone. Wears glasses. From the look of her calves, she does a bit of jogging. And she's got a nice pair of tits on her too.'

Our Herman, crawling out from under the table with his fag end: 'And you can add to that, she's wearing white knickers!'

'You prick, are you sure? Shit, that's three crates of beer for fuck's sake.'

My father again: 'Is it that woman from last night?'

'Hey, lady, are you that woman from last night?'

The lady did not say a word.

'P., she won't answer that question.'

'I told her to leave me alone.'

'Hey, lady, our P. says you have to leave him alone.'

But the lady just stayed sitting where she was sitting, imperturbable, determined.

'P, she's not budging. Come downstairs, lad, and work it out yourself!'

'She's not fucking pregnant, is she?'

'What do I care? If you want to know if she's pregnant or not, you'll have to drag yourself out of bed and ask her yourself. I've done my bit.'

'Wait. I'm coming.'

'He's on his way.'

'On his way' was overstating things. Before we saw him appear in the living room in just his underpants and his grey post office vest, my father first spent ten minutes leaning over a hankie to hawk up the green globs that I now also, unfortunately, but with a deep disdain for death, cough up after waking. But I still don't come anywhere near the groans with which my father dredged the traces of tar up out of his lungs every morning, that day too, or the retching noises that signalled the start of his day.

Without deigning to look at anyone, he walked straight through to the toilet, where he pissed into the bowl from a good two feet away with the door open, grimacing painfully all the while and pressing his ribcage with one hand as if trying to squeeze out a kidney. Only then did he turn back to the living room, still in his underpants, on which he had now leaked, light up a cigarette and ask, 'Where's this woman who's come to see me?'

We pointed at the coffee table.

'I don't know *her*. Are you taking the piss or what?'

The lady finally stood up, walked over to my father, held out a hand and said, 'Mr Verhulst, I'm Nelly Fockedey of the Special Youth Welfare Service and I've come to see what kind of surroundings and conditions you're raising your son in.'

There was nothing wrong with the way I was being raised – where did that bitch get the gall to stick her beak into it? Her being sent here by the juvenile court only made the conspiracy theories worse. The Special Youth Welfare Service only got called in when they'd been

89

tipped off. If we ever found out who had complained about our family, the blabbermouth would do better to leave the country. Special Youth Welfare, for fuck's sake, they took your kids away, our Herman knew all about that. They gave your little ones to a fucking-cunt-of-a-bloody-fucking foster family or put them in a home or sent them to a boarding school and sentenced you for neglect as if you were halfway to being a bloody child abuser.

Jesus fucking Christ.

Mother of fucking God.

The woman was walking around our house, noting precisely what she saw. In the bedroom she saw the ashtrays, the piles of clothes and the piss buckets we'd forgotten to empty. And she can't have missed the anti-crab cream on the bedside table and the bottles under the bed.

'Does the boy sleep in here?'

'Where else is he going to sleep? Are you in the habit of putting your kids to bed in the coal shed perhaps?'

'Where's he study?'

I didn't study, but when I wanted to make out I was studying, I did it at the kitchen table. 'What's wrong with that?'

Our Girder whisked away a pair of frilly knickers.

'Why doesn't the child live with his mother?'

'You'll have to ask him that yourself!'

'Wouldn't you prefer to live with your mum?'

I didn't answer.

'Tell me a little about your mother.'

I didn't answer.

'Miss Fockedey, his mother's a whore!'
'I asked the boy, not you!'
'My mother's a whore.'

A little about my mother?

Like a journalist showing off his newly acquired press card or a child running into the yard with a good report held up like a banner to salute the endless summer holiday, my mother waddled in one day with her pee pass. It had taken a lot of bureaucratic hassle, doctor's appointments and tests in which cold bars and rods were inserted into the cavities of my prehistory, but finally she had it, her pee pass, and she immediately put it up on the mantelpiece, next to the holy cards and the Virgin Mary under the glass dome she dusted every Friday.

A pee pass gives its owner the right to piddle in public facilities whenever he or she pleases and is only allocated on medical grounds. An attractive document, it was coloured yellow – either by accident or design – and carried the owner's name, address, signature, date of birth and a photo. As far as our family knew, there was only one photo of my mother with a smile on her face, and that was on her pee pass. She'd rushed off to the photographer specially to get it, but not without visiting the hairdresser and dentist first. Her moustache didn't make it through the day unscathed either.

Removing my mother's moustache was an enormous operation

that always made me think of a religious rite in a country I don't ever want to visit. She heated wax in a big pan on the stove until it was flexible enough, then smeared that wax on a rag and laid the rag between her nose and upper lip, leaving it there for a good twenty minutes until the wax had penetrated all the way to the roots of her moustache hairs and set hard. The idea was to rip all of those hairs out of her skin in one go by giving the rag a quick tug, which naturally hurt like hell and required courage. And that was the problem. My mother had a horror of self-inflicted pain. More than once she spent a whole day with that rag under her nose – even doing the shopping with it stuck there because she knew no shame, the only thing she was ashamed of was her son – until she gathered up enough courage to tear the tash off her face. Often, realizing that she was no masochist, she turned to me for help, asking me – I was a lazy slug, after all, and never did anything without being asked – to mercilessly pull that piece of cloth off her face. She didn't want me to hesitate or think about it, I just had to give the rag one hard jerk and rip it off her lip. And I did. Gladly. She lost her moustache and I got to take out some of my frustration, so we were both happy; it was a win–win situation and I too can take some of the credit for my mother appearing contented and de-moustachioed on her pee pass.

All the things that made my mother unhappy were related to me, sometimes very directly. Her leaving wet chairs behind her and sometimes realizing to her own astonishment that she was soaked down to her socks was no exception. Apparently I gave her a pretty hard time when I was born. Even less wanted than the pregnancy was the labour, which would have dragged on for days, determined as I was to be born after my own expiry date, if the surgeon hadn't stuck his scalpel into my mother and brought me into the world through another, more spacious hole. But the damage I caused to my mother's gynaecological plumbing was enormous, catastrophic in fact. Besides making her completely unattractive to my own father through my birth, I had also rearranged her insides (if you live somewhere nine months, you're bound to start moving the furniture; as far as I'm concerned that's the most normal thing in the world) and helped to permanently ruin her urinary tract.

What she initially called a 'chill on the bladder' turned out to be nothing less than incontinence, albeit at an early stage.

My mother could give me a very reproachful look when she'd just peed on the kitchen floor again.

The last thing my father installed before he left her was a drain in the middle of the living room. It came in very handy.

My mother replaced the photo of my father in her purse with the pee pass so that she'd always have it with her in case of emergency.

My mother was a skinflint who washed out and saved every mustard or roll-mop jar in case she ever needed it. Our cellar was crammed with glass jars; it was impossible for one human to fill a supply like that with things like jam in one lifetime. And my mother would never fill a single jar with jam, because homemade jam was dearer than jam from the jam factory, so she kept buying factory jam and getting more glass jars to wash out and keep. At least if a war broke out we wouldn't run short of jars, we could count on that. But stinginess expands into all facets of a mother's life, and her pee pass too was something to deploy in her battle against waste. We couldn't even get on a bus without her asking the driver if her pee pass made her eligible for a concession. At a theatre or cinema box office she would fish all kinds of cards up out of her handbag and the pee pass trumped the lot. It stopped people in their tracks and they would often give her a discount to put an end to her moaning. She was the kind of person who saw obtaining reductions as a sport, a lifestyle, and she would never really be happy until she had been classified as a handicapped OAP student. That was the pinnacle for my mother, being disadvantaged to the value of three cumulative discounts, and it's probably the only one of her dreams I would have gladly seen fulfilled.

If we happened to be out driving somewhere when she felt the waters pounding against the ruptured dam of her sphincters, she would call a sanitary stop at a petrol station. Before she got her pee pass that had been out of the question because petrol stations always made you pay for the use of the facilities. Instead she would order me to stand in front of the first bush she came to on the side of the road and yell if anyone approached. When she'd finished peeing and had wiped her privates with a few blades of grass, I had to pick the pine needles out of her hairdo. But a pee pass grants you free entry to the loos of any establishment whatsoever, and although it only saved a pittance each time, my mother still pulled it out at every opportunity. A card-carrying member of the pissers' association, my father said. A lack of tact, according to some; a sense of humour, as far as I was concerned. Rather than spend a penny, my mother aimed her index finger at me like a pistol and told the toilet attendant all about the havoc I had wreaked on her body.

I hated her and resolved to run away.

Somewhere in the treaties about the rights of the child there must be an article with a convoluted affirmation of the juvenile's right to be protected from bitches of mothers. Toerags of mothers. Shockers of mothers. Beasts of mothers. Mothers. I was convinced that a magnificent future was awaiting me in a home somewhere. Or else I could go to my father's and stay there. Either way, I'd had it with making origami flowers at school for Mother's Day, I'd folded my last piece of paper for that snake.

Our annual day trip to the sea seemed the ideal occasion for me to carry out my plan.

Ostend beach on a summer's day. The moment she was lying face down, roasting in the sun and assuming that I was collecting shells near the water's edge, I would make a run for it. Long before she felt the slightest suspicion that I might have met a tragic death by drowning, I would be at my father's or with a foster family.

But for some reason I've never been able to fathom, my mother only wanted to tan her front that year. It is true though – a brown back is not really that much use to you when all you do with it is stand in front of a mirror, and my mother sat up straight with two knitting needles and a ball of grey wool, knitting away at yet another ugly jumper she'd force me to wear, keeping constant watch and ready to leap into action if I disappeared out of sight.

I had built two sandcastles that could hold back the Moors but not the tide when my mother beckoned. She had to pee.

'Pee here!' I said. 'Nobody'll notice.' I was all ready to dig a hole in the sand with my spade when a slap in the face calmed me down and convinced me to accompany her up to the promenade where there were public toilets, but such long queues that I knew that yet another public humiliation awaited me. And yes, my mother started waving her pee pass around and calling to all and sundry, 'Hello, excuse me. Attention please, everyone. I have a pee pass. I have a right to go first.'

And me, forced to stand there holding my mother's hand. The earth didn't crack open, there was no chasm for me to sink into. I dragged myself through my umpteenth embarrassment.

Although . . . Justice occurred. Not one of those beachgoers-cum-toiletgoers stepped aside to let her go first. There was mumbling and grumbling, an extended listen-lady-we've-been-standing-here-half-an-hour-with-our-legs-crossed-too. If they'd taken a photo of me in that moment, I'd have finally had one of me with a grin on my face too.

'What now?' she asked.

'Pee in the sea!' I said.

'In the sea?'

Didn't the woman know where the filth that flowed through our sewers ended up?

My mother put on the embossed bathing cap that made her look like her head had been wallpapered, felt the temperature of the water repeatedly with her big toe, then waded into the sea. This was my chance to run and I took it.

The last I saw of my mother she was up to her chin in the water, eyes shut, holding her pee pass in the air with her left hand, and adding her contribution to the immeasurable emptiness of the oceans.

The Pilgrim

We were at the intersection of two events – according to some of literature's most eminent figures, *the* place where Great Stories should be situated – and wondered for a split second on the back seat of our Girder's white second-hand Alfa Romeo how these events had changed each other during their improbable coincidence. Two facts, each separate, but seeking each other's presence with such spine-chilling timing that one could only wonder if they hadn't somehow evoked each other, if they weren't both parts of what I now call: the conspiracy of destiny.

We: that was my father, our Herman, our Girder and me.

And the events that intersected so impressively one Saturday in March were these: my father was on the point of booking himself into the Pilgrim, a specialist drying-out clinic that was infamous in our circles – having jettisoned all doubt, he had thrown open the door of the Alfa Romeo to stride into the icy building where they would keep him away from alcohol for months on end; we had asked him for the last time if he was sure of his decision and he had answered, 'Yes!' – and in that very instant, not a moment before or a moment after, a despairing patient threw himself out of a third-floor window of that very same drying-out clinic. Arms and legs spread wide, face aimed courageously at the ground that would finish the job.

There had been nothing to foreshadow my father's decision. He woke late, joined us at the table and said, 'You have to take me into rehab today. I can't go on.'

We knew that thoughts come at night, in bed, and we suspected that my father had lain awake in mortal fear, feeling the pain in his body, in his liver, his stomach, his chest. And that he, alone with his thoughts, lost his brave acceptance of physical deterioration. We couldn't exclude the possibility that he had licked his sopping hands, discovering to his horror that he had started to sweat alcohol, that his body was defeated and no longer knew how to get rid of all that fluid, that it had started to leak it out of all possible pores and holes. My father now tasted like beer and his armpits smelled like it too. Maybe he had already noticed the whites of his eyes growing yellow, his steady loss of weight. A drinker's coffin is seldom a heavy burden, undertakers are always glad to carry them, and our family would have saved a lot of money if we'd been able to pay for our funerals by the pound. Did he think that night about the worms that were besotted by the deliciously fermenting bodies of dead soaks and made the soil of our graveyard so rich that the gravediggers spent their working hours growing carrots and spinach between the collapsed and forgotten tombstones of a previous generation of chain drinkers?

He couldn't go on. We looked at him with the silent disbelief we no longer bothered to show the smokers who blandly asserted that they had given up cancer sticks for good only to stride into the boozer the next day with a big cigar between their teeth.

Almost indifferently, we listened to his absolutely worthless resolution. A whim, that was what it was, the primitive reaction of a hypochondriac who was afraid of dying and had suffered bursts of anxiety during a short night in a clammy bed. The seriousness of his decision would be shown up the moment he laid eyes on a freshly tapped beer. Our Devil. People believed in God, but at least the Devil believed in us. We had to maintain him, that Devil, and my father would definitely go back to doing just that the moment he had recovered from his doom mongering. All we had to do was wait for him to get thirsty and rediscover the complete inadequacy of water. Right now he couldn't go on. Right now he didn't want to go on. For now.

He was shaking and couldn't get the lighter up to his mouth. I lit his cigarette, sucked the flame into it and handed it back to him. His first deep drag tore the paper of his St Michel non-filter and after he'd cleared his throat three times the wet strands of tobacco were still hanging from his lower lip. He was a clumsy child who let his son pick the tobacco off his lip, and gradually we realized that it was true, he really couldn't go on. He was a wreck, it had taken a toll, this person had to go in for a complete overhaul.

'You sure, P.?'

To never drink again, never, ever, ever. And really meaning it, never. That horrific word: never. *Nie. Jamais. Nooit. Jamás.*

Surely he didn't mean it.

But he grabbed the phone book, looked up the number of the

clinic and called to ask if he could be admitted that day. It was Saturday, he was told, beds were in short supply, they didn't even open the door unless it was an emergency. 'I am an emergency!' my father snarled and we saw that there was no manipulation or tactics behind that statement at all. At five o'clock that Saturday afternoon, my father would be able to admit himself to the in-our-circles-highly-infamous detoxification clinic, the Pilgrim in Scheldewindeke. A sympathetic tear rolled down his mother's cheek and she gave my dad such a long hug that everyone who saw it felt uncomfortable.

'Fine,' said Girder, who had just got his driving licence and somewhere, God knows where, found the money to immediately acquire a second-hand Alfa. 'If that's what you really want, I'll take you.'

'I'll come too,' said Herman.

And so, taking my father to the drying-out clinic came to resemble something of an excursion.

He stuffed some underpants and socks, clean shirts, cigarettes and a couple of tracksuit bottoms into his bright red sports bag. Aftershave was forbidden because it contained alcohol. It wouldn't be the first time someone had cracked open a bottle of eau de Cologne to celebrate having nothing to celebrate. He seemed to be ready and we left. The next time he entered this house he'd be a totally different person and we'd have to do our best to even recognize him.

The drive from Arsendegem to Scheldewindeke was long and above all ugly, but strewn with pubs. We'd only just turned the corner, waving to my elated grandmother like retards in a bus, when my father revealed his plan to get completely shit-faced one last time. The very last time. Really, the very last time and then never, never, never again. Just for the symbolism, the ritual of it, we would honour every pub between Arsendegem and Scheldewindeke with a visit, and my uncles were up for it. Civilization is lost once people lose their respect for ritual. My uncles must have been gratified by the proposal my father put to them, at least partly. Because if my father had realized that he needed help to get off the booze, they could expect to suffer the same insight in the near future. That's why they were glad to see how greedily my father planted his moustache in the head of his beer that afternoon and relieved to note the gleam in his eye as he tipped the amber fluid down his throat at a rate that could be seen as a sporting achievement. Ten pubs and twice as many beers later, neither my uncles nor my father seemed to remember the purpose of the outing. It was just the usual sociable Saturday, driving from one pub to another. A kind of pilgrimage. In the Blue Bayou they even found time for a game of pool, and somewhere in Wetteren we were kind enough to make up the desired number of players for a game of darts. All as per usual.

It was half past four when it suddenly became necessary to resort to violence to round off a discussion in the Station, and our Girder was about to take the duty upon himself when my father said, 'Guys, it's gone half four. It's time.'

He was serious. He had drunk his last glass of beer without any kind of theatricality. We hadn't even seen him drink it, let alone taken a photo of the historic moment. Father with glass. Always good for a laugh later as the portrait on his headstone.

Of course, our Girder would have much rather stayed in the pub for the fight he himself had provoked, and we were forced to endure the shame of being called cowards for leaving just when the challenged giant had taken off his jacket to lay into him. You didn't do that, scarper when it was time for a punch-up. *We* didn't do it. We let a perfect opportunity to permanently establish our name and reputation in Wetteren slip, climbed into the car indignantly and drove without a word to Scheldewindeke, pulling into the drying-out clinic's car park at ten to five.

THE PILGRIM PSYCHIATRIC CLINIC it said.

'Is this it, P.?'

'This is it!'

'But that's a psychiatric clinic. That's for loonies.'

'This is it, I tell you. Fucking believe me once in your fucking life!'

We gaped at the immense building that must have started out as a monastery or boarding school and saw that it satisfied the architectural precepts for a place dedicated to the highly efficient production of human misery.

Frumpish women, shabby children, skinny men in tracksuits and other similar individuals left the building's right wing and waved at the top-floor windows, behind which pathetic figures answered the waving hands with flaccid smiles and teeth of frosted glass. Visiting had apparently just ended. In the weeks to come it would be my father standing there at a window waving a limp hand. And it would be us sitting with him in a visitors' room full of whining brats and humming Coke machines, enquiring about the successes he had already chalked up in his life as an insipid teetotaller. It would be us finding him bloated and pudge-faced, pretending to believe him when he said he was glad he'd finally purged the filth from his body. Totally trivial but good to know: there was a timeless inevitability to the harrowing scene that had played out before our eyes of visitors heading off home and leaving lonely patients, who were forced to save up the rest of their stories until next week's visiting hour.

'You sure, P.? You really want to go in there? We can always turn around and go home.'

Herman whipped a bottle of cheap jenever out from under the passenger seat and handed it to my dad. 'Here, lad, get some of this into you before you go inside. The last one. To get it out of your system.'

The bottle did a round, uniting our thoughts, which we didn't pin down but left to drift through our minds along with all the other thoughts that had been drifting through our minds for years.

'You do know what they're going to do to you in there, P.? Next thing you know they'll be up you with their rubber gloves. Poking a finger around in your arse to make sure you're not trying to smuggle anything in.'

'That's right, P. And then they'll stick you in a tiny cubicle for three days' quarantine. They'll pump you full of pills and strap you down on a bed. Because starting tomorrow you're in detox, that's what they call it, detox, and then you're going to see little bugs crawling all over the wardrobe and there might not even be a wardrobe in there. You're going to shout and scream and kick and lash out and they're going to leave you lying there as long as it takes until you calm down and feel better and ask them for a bite to eat.'

'You sure, P.? Do you really want to go in there? Because after three days you'll get a room of your own. A tiny little room where you can hang up a poster to make you feel at home. And they'll play games with you as if you're a little kid again. Football and softball and hide-and-seek. And every evening, a quiz. About film stars one day, capital cities the next.'

'Yeah, P., and sometimes they'll stick a paintbrush in your hand and you'll get to varnish chairs or something like that. Occupational therapy, they call it. Everything inside that building's therapy. They'll make you shout your name out loud to regain your self-esteem. That's what they call it, self-esteem. And you'll go and stand there in some psychologist's office. "Pierre, Pierre, Pierre," you'll start shouting. You'll shout your own fucking name to prove you love yourself and, worst of all, they won't tolerate you feeling ridiculous while you're at it. Do you really want to go in there, P.? Are you sure?'

'That's right. And it will be three months, P., three whole months, I tell you, before they let you come back home again. For two lousy days. And during those two days, you won't be allowed to touch a drop or else they'll strap you down on that iron bed again with those same leather straps and stick those same rubber fingers up your arse and the whole pantomime will start all over again. Until you can't bear the sight of beer. Until you can't bear the smell of beer. Until you puke your guts up if you even hear the word beer. Do you think you're up to that, P., puking when you hear the word beer?'

'Are you sure, P.? Is this really what you want, lad?'

'Yes,' he said, grabbing the sports bag with his paltry possessions and throwing open the car door, ready for the biggest challenge a man can take upon himself.

That was when it happened. That was when the two events intersected.

We could well imagine the life of the man who had thrown himself from the third floor: his despair giving way to determination as, arms and legs spread, facing the ground, he hit the cement of the car park without uttering a cry. The wave of spasms that passed through his body was no more than a shudder, and that showed how tired of life he must have been. Even his shudder couldn't keep going for more than one short second. He too must have once entered this building ready to fight for a life free of addiction. And gradually he'd realized that it wasn't possible, that over the years his whole being had become synonymous with alcohol, dope or whatever; he couldn't do without. He was no longer capable of living in the pure body he had inhabited in early childhood, a body that could hardly remember its long-departed guest. That was why he was lying there now with blood trickling out of his ear.

My father too must have had these thoughts in that moment.

We looked at each other, his hand was still on the car-door handle.

'Look after our Dimmy while I'm away. Promise?'

And he was gone. A puny little man with a red sports bag full of worn-out underwear and odd socks disappeared through the big doors he wouldn't see the outside of for at least three months. The enormous, icy building swallowed him whole. Soon he'd have to make some new little friends.

'We'll write, P. Long letters.' But he was already gone and didn't hear the lie.

Meanwhile all kinds of people had rushed out to surround the warm body. You couldn't tell whether they were addicts or doctors, and we found that quite gratifying. The bed shortage had been resolved, temporarily at least, and it was quite possible that after his period of quarantine my father would be allocated the room of the man who had just jumped. Hmm. The beat goes on.

'Now what?' Herman asked, clearly shaken.

'Back to Wetteren,' snapped Girder. 'We've got a bone to pick with someone in the Station.'

The Collector

'My father said I'm not allowed to play with you any more,' Frankie admitted on a day that saw my outlook on life firm up a little.

Play? The word alone.

Frankie was the only and probably very welcome son of one of the families that bought up the last land in Arsendegem to fill it with the villas that were still seen in those days as the benchmark for happiness. Brick boxes with a drive leading to the garage. These symmetrical houses all had hedges to keep the owners' lives hidden from us as much as possible and give them something to trim in summer to satisfy their predilection for orderliness. The letterboxes were a short walk from the front door: at one the postman had to drop the packages into a barrel held by an angelic nudist, another boasted a construction that he took for a work of art instead of a letterbox, laying the newspapers on the doorstep as a result. The newcomers had dogs they trusted so much they'd installed alarm systems on their front walls and brick barbecues that took pride of place on the manicured lawns in their gardens. Some of them had ponds with goldfish and fountains, ponds they covered with wire mesh because they were afraid their children might fall in and drown. On Saturdays the owners of all this opulence attacked their cars with a garden hose or demonstrated the noise of their lawnmowers. They also had verandas around the back where, if it was good weather and the hedge had been newly coiffed, you might catch a glimpse of a woman doing the ironing while watching TV.

They were families without roots, born somewhere and raised nowhere in particular. They didn't have any bond to Arsendegem at all: their having come here to live was related solely to the available land and how it had grown more and more expensive and harder to find in the cities. Not one of them had dropped by to introduce themselves as our new neighbours, they didn't come to our parties or pubs, they never participated in anything. They shunned the annual fairs and, unlike us, deposited their money safely in the bank, never dropping it into the pub's slate club until there was enough to blow in one very short evening. You saw them giving us dubious looks when we made our traditional drunken return from a game of fives, or racing inside with fright when we kicked our cheating wives in the crotch or hurled items of furniture out to smash on the cobbles. But if someone had made a TV series about us they would have watched it with amusement.

'And why's that?'

'Why's what?'

'Why is it that you're not allowed to be seen with me any more?'

'Your father's mad. He's locked up in a psychiatric hospital.'

'And my mother's a whore, Frankie. Didn't your daddy tell you that too? My mother's a whore and I'm the bastard son she threw out on the street. Your father doesn't know the half of it.'

'He said you're a lesser sort. Weaklings. If your kind wasn't kept artificially alive by social security, you'd have rotted away long ago. In the wild you wouldn't stand a chance: stronger species would have wiped you out to maintain the balance. The Verhulsts booze. The Verhulsts get into fights and live off the state. They're exploiters and parasites. Don't get angry at *me*. I'm just telling you what my father says, I don't say it myself.'

I wasn't angry. As if I gave a shit about not being allowed to be seen together any more. It was Frankie's problem, not mine. He was dull. Not overly dense for somebody who, when you looked at it closely, had also descended from a monkey, true, but there was nothing to him. He had no character, neither good nor bad. Unless I was very much mistaken, I was the only one of his peers who sought him out now and then. Frankie would never have anything going for him, I saw that at a glance. Socially he would go completely off the rails, specializing in computers or something like that, and pine away without ever having known the true blessings of loneliness. He'd been going down that path for a while now, it seemed to me. He didn't know a thing about football, and the grandeur of bike racing was beyond him. Sitting on the pavement when girls who were always just a little bit too old for us passed by, he didn't even notice the difference between a bum and a world-class arse. Music was lost on him, he didn't read, he thought cigarettes were bad for your health – the guy was hopeless. The only thing that seemed to get him through his days on earth was, typically, his collection.

It's possible that numerous studies have been published on the subject, and I vaguely remember reading somewhere that collectors enjoy having power over others. They are unstable people who, unable to control their lives, compensate by ruling over a collection of something or other. What they collect is irrelevant. It could be stamps or beer mats, cigar bands or army helmets. A total lack of affinity with the thing they happen to collect is one of the essential characteristics of collectors. My Uncle Girder, for instance, now that we've broached the subject, collected pubic hair. But it would be out of order to claim that Uncle Girder was a collector. His personal bond with the object was too great. He just happened to snip a small lock off the girls he'd done it with, stick it in an album and note the girl's name and the date of the trim under the tuft of hair. That was all. It would have never occurred to Girder to start swapping pubic hair with other pube collectors, simply because if he did there would no longer be any bond between him and his collection. You could call him a souvenir hound, the self-satisfied and megalomaniac designer of his own hunting trophies, but never a collector. Because if you called our Girder a collector, you'd have to expect stamp collectors to limit themselves to stamps that were stuck to letters that were addressed to them personally, and collectors of cigar bands would only own bands from cigars they themselves had smoked. You could never acquire enough power over a particular object if you had to have a personal bond with it.

Each object needed to be interchangeable and there had to be duplicates to peddle at collectors' meets.

Frankie collected model trains made by the Märklin company. Completely unoriginal, but that too is in the nature of a collector. They have to be able to measure themselves against other collectors. There are countless numbers of objects, but all real collections come down to a hundred or so basic items. Because a real collector always collects something that masses of other drips collect too. I'm sure a biologist could provide a humorous explanation.

The models Frankie collected were replicas of locomotive engines, carriages and wagons from pre-nineteen-forty-something. Frankie had never travelled on those trains, by which I mean the original versions: that overly fastidious father of his had probably never been in one of those carriages either. They were beautiful, of course, those little trains. You'll never hear me claim otherwise. And each one cost a fortune, so they assured me. It didn't seem particularly difficult to amass a collection of Märklin trains: apart from a few exclusive models, they were all available in shops or at special exhibitions organized by the Märklin company, and whoever spent the most money immediately had the most beautiful collection. Whatever else you could say about it – that it was crass, tasteless, juvenile or typical macho behaviour – collecting pubic hair was a democratic hobby. The Verhulsts were pro-democracy, always had been.

Frankie had set up his own miniature world in the cellar of their villa. That was the big difference between him and me: I slept in the same room as my father and uncles, he had an entire cellar to himself to dedicate to his hobby.

A gigantic network of railway tracks was stuck to thick, high-quality boards. The trains thundered through tunnels and over tiny little bridges. There were functioning signals and gates and train stations with minuscule station clocks. There were mountains with scree slopes and tree lines, lush green valleys grazed by perfect replica cows with perfect replica udders, canals and lakes with yachts and fishermen. Two trains never crashed into each other. Not even for a laugh. That was what I would have done if I'd owned a railway network like that: I'd have had the trains derailing and crashing into each other, and desperate little figures would hurl themselves in front of the trains after impeccably staged scenes with their lovers. Things like that. To have a bit of fun. Not Frankie. He was the absolute sovereign and supreme commander of an imitation world that ran more perfectly than its archetype. Everything was on time. The slightest hitch or tiniest delay would have dismayed him and had him penning furious letters to the Märklin customer service department. But still, it was his hobby, not mine.

Whenever he had a new carriage or engine he would invite – I should say, beg – me to have a look in his cellar. The only problem that had to be won over was their dog, Harrar, a hideous creature, but that wasn't its fault, of course. That made two dogs I had to watch out for. Not just Palmier's bitch, which still hadn't been found and would definitely tear my throat out if she ever tracked me down, but Harrar too, who had a natural aversion to me and was, unfortunately, in much better shape than Palmier's pathetic quadruped. A male. Harrar seemed to have been trained to turn bloodthirsty the moment he saw me, but once he'd been paid off with a large, juicy steak and taken it into his kennel, I could enter the residence with immunity and Frankie would drag me down to his cellar. Brimming with pride, he showed me his new locomotive and brought me up to date on all the details of this particular series number, information I deliberately blocked out while nodding the nod of the interested and making Frankie the happiest twerp for miles around. But that was over now, because nobody else would come and see his collection: with me, he had exhausted the entire stock of altruists and social workers in his circle of acquaintance.

'Don't be angry at me. It's my father. Really. He's scared you'll teach me to smoke and drink and stuff. And steal. I have to stick to my own kind.'

'I'm not angry at you, Frankie.' I was starting to get sick of the little wimp. 'Really, I understand. You and your father are two completely separate things. But I'm not sure how well you know *us*.'

'What do you mean?'

'Us, the Verhulsts. If your father knows the Verhulsts that well, he must know that a Verhulst never stands alone.'

He didn't understand; maybe he was dense after all.

'You can't drive a wedge between us. We always stick up for each other. We're kind of old-fashioned that way, Frankie. Do you understand that word, Frankie, old-fashioned? Sense of honour, that kind of thing. Ever heard of it? You'll figure it out soon enough when my Uncle Girder is smashing your face in. You mustn't get angry at me,

Frankie. It's my uncle. Really. My uncle and not me. They'll do your father too. After all, he called *my* father mad. You do appreciate that something like that's not on, we have to stick up for our good name. And that lapdog of yours, Harrar, we'll think of something for him too. That's more up my Uncle Heavy's street, he's good with dogs. He'll have some fun.'

Into karate and bodybuilding at the time, Uncle Heavy was starting to take up more and more space. He shredded telephone books with his bare hands, chopped bricks in half and swallowed tablets with unique vitamins. To accentuate his muscles, he'd lie for hours under solarium lamps with his cowboy paperbacks. Soon he'd be able to take part in competitions and rent himself out as a racy act for hen nights where girls wanted to let their hair down and give in to their animal instincts for one last night, unashamedly delighting in a hunk of firm, well-toasted flesh, and it was a pleasure to have him as an uncle. If someone so much as laid a finger on me, all I had to do was say I was going to tell my Uncle Heavy. From the look on Frankie's face, he understood the implications very well.

There's nothing bad about people disappearing out of our lives. Recently I reached the point in my life at which I'd scrawled on every available page in my address book. I remember the awe I felt as a young man for people with well-filled address books and chaotic agendas. They had a life. They had so much life they couldn't remember it all and had to organize their circle of friends according to the principles of good bookkeeping. I don't think I bought my first diary until I was twenty-five, and when I finally had one I didn't need to consult it because my memory was better than my social life. Gradually I began to see my diary as a logbook of the unoccurred and essentially it's remained that to this day: full of appointments that will be rescheduled later and finally cancelled, which is something I seldom regret. An address book only became necessary when my friends systematically and more or less inevitably gave in to gentrification, acquiring things like telephones, faxes and even Internet connections. The good old days, really, for someone like me who has difficulty remembering numbers, because by now they all have at least two telephones, which are often simultaneously engaged and ask me to leave a message after a long piece of boring music and a beep.

Anyway, suddenly that address book was full. I bought a new one, larger, and resolved to start by meticulously transcribing all of the addresses from the old one. Two address books are too awkward for me. I know what I'm like, I'd always try to look up an address or telephone number in the wrong one first. That was when I made my discovery. Address books are full of people you once knew: some well, some too well. My best friend appeared several times, but that was his fault for never sticking it out for more than three years with a woman, moving so often that when he, strangely enough, suddenly got married, we bought him a sixth-hand caravan. If you mix with people like that, your address book can fill up very quickly. I don't maintain any contacts with people whose surname starts with Z and have never seen that as a shortcoming, but between the names Abrassart and Ysewyn there was a long series of people I hadn't seen for years and would probably never see again and I wasn't bothered. There is nothing bad about people disappearing out of our lives, and I immediately stopped transcribing all those names and addresses.

An address that I did have in my new address book was Frankie's. Strange because he, of course, had never made it into the first edition of my list of friends. When he handed me the card with the address that I would later copy into my new address book, more or less twenty years had passed since we had last spoken and, yes, that was the time he explained to me that his father had forbidden him from associating with riff-raff.

Our coincidental encounter took place in the small town of Chiny, where I had come to check out the story-telling festival they held there annually with ever-increasing success. The entire town centre was strewn with beer tents and bookstalls. There were stands where you could buy T-shirts printed with moronic slogans and Chilean llama-wool shoulder bags (complete with accompanying panpipe players). On a street corner a crowd had gathered to listen to someone sing a Portuguese fado in a voice that was truly terrible and with a sorrow that was transparently fake. Local artists had transformed their garages into galleries, hanging canvases covered with artistic splashes and smudges above the tyres and cans of oil. And in between times the public could pop into a hayshed or classroom to listen to professional storytellers who had been flown in all the way from Africa or Australia just for this festival. Not my kind of event, and I was already walking back to the car to pursue my life more successfully at home on the sofa when I spotted Frankie in the mob. Ugly people are easier to recognize than beauties, and although he had still been a beardless teenybopper the last time I saw him, no one could convince me that this man could be anyone but Frankie. It was obvious that he had remained a collector all this time: I saw him picking through trays that were a goldmine for some and a garbage bin for others. Besides soggy newspapers for the masses of bibliophiles that had turned up, the stall-holder was flogging other curiosities, things like small plastic Smurfs from the 1970s. Smurfs as lawyers, bricklayers and nurses. Papa Smurf as a magician, Smurfs on surfboards, Smurfs playing electric guitar – they had once been included as a free gift in a box of a particular brand of cheese spread. A Smurf for every person, that must have been the idea in the seventies, and thirty years later people started collecting the crap. Besides Smurfs, festival visitors who didn't know what to do with their money could also buy Spike and Suzy dolls, Walt Disney figurines and other gewgaws for the eternally infantile. Although it's a proven fact that curiosity is a source of much misery, one doesn't always need to take that into account and so, wondering at the purpose of Frankie's search, I headed over to the stall myself and started rummaging through one of the trays. It was probably a hotbed of microbes, but so be it.

'How much is this one?' I asked the vendor, holding a Smurf up in the light. A cheerful Smurf with a red nose and a big beer stein in one hand.

'Four euros.'

'Four euros? For a Smurf that's drinking flat German beer?'

'It's a one-off,' he said.

'But it's made in Taiwan. It says so on the sole of the shoe. "Made in Taiwan". Child labour, probably.'

'Four euros. That's the price.'

I bought the Smurf, which now stands on my desk, but not to start a collection.

By raising all that racket I'd managed to attract Frankie's attention, and that, of course, was my plan.

'Hey,' he said, 'aren't you . . .'

'Well, if it's not Frankie,' I said. 'Has your father decided to let you talk to me yet?' And I could tell from the awkward smile on his face that the creature had a memory. He ignored the question, which in his position was the most advisable way of being rude, and I braced myself to hear that it had been a bloody long time, but wasn't yet fully braced when he said, 'Man, it's been a bloody long time.'

It depended on what you considered long. I've known days that passed with the utmost difficulty, I've seen the hands of the clock revolve around each other with sadistic reluctance often enough, like two lovers playfully postponing their little death, but the twenty years between two encounters with Frankie had been a sigh. My attitude reminded me again of how rude I can be, a grudge bearer, incapable of forgiving, furious at everyone who has ever declared war on me, no matter how fleetingly. It's a character trait, not my most appealing, but I engrave the name of anyone who's ever bumped my car on the list that includes Frankie's. 'Man, it's been a bloody long time,' he said, and I felt again that I could accept nothing less than his complete destruction. What if I worked down that list, making everyone with an outstanding debt settle up their account with me, starting right away with Frankie? I would make him pay his debt to my father – and my uncles while I was at it, I still had that much sense of honour. He had called them the dregs of the sewers, my father a madman; I couldn't allow that. What if I publicly humiliated Frankie right there and then? But despite the impression I might have accidentally given here, I'm not always that smug about my character, and instead I spontaneously suggested going for a beer. That's my misfortune, I often suggest things I don't feel like at all and it's only rarely that people sense that I don't mean it when I ask them if they feel like going for a drink to catch up on the years that have passed irretrievably beyond our reach, making it impossible for us to ever go back to do a few things better the second time round. Asking them if they want to go for a drink is simply my awkward way of fobbing people off without rubbing their noses in it. So there I was, sitting at a table in a beer tent with Frankie.

'Still a collector, I see.'

'Once a collector, always a collector,' he said.

'What are you into now?' I asked, because that's how conversation works: someone says he's a collector and deliberately refrains from going on to say what he collects, so that the other person can ask what he collects.

'I'm into Judaica these days.'

'Judaica?'

'Judaica,' he repeated. 'Things that are related to Judaism. Skullcaps, candelabras, you know.'

Yeah, of course I knew. I was just surprised to hear the word on his lips. Judaica, how did he come up with something like that? Since Frankie, I had obviously met other people who built up collections, of glass owls, for instance, and I always wondered how they had struck on the idea of starting up. Had they received a glass owl as a gift one day and been so blown away by it that they immediately wanted a thousand glass owls? What was the process? Do people sometimes accidentally buy an extra cupboard and then need to fill it up? Can someone wake up one morning and suddenly say, 'Starting today, I collect Jewish stuff'?

'Of course, you have to narrow a collection like that down,' he continued, clearly assuming that I didn't see the subject of conversation as concluded. 'By limiting yourself you make your collection more distinctive, stronger. Of course, I could just collect everything that falls under the heading of Judaica: skullcaps, candelabra, old editions of the Torah, Kosher cookbooks, the whole caboodle, but it wouldn't be much fun. No hunting involved.'

'A-ha,' I said, panicking slightly as I ascertained that there was hardly enough tobacco left in my pouch to get me through the conversation with my fingernails intact. 'You limit yourself to the skullcaps?'

'No,' he said, continuing his mediocre exposition. 'I collect figurines of Jews. Actually, small figurines, to be precise.'

'And they exist?' I said, feigning fascination. Odd that I never thought of becoming a psychologist!

'Definitely, they exist all right. You just have to search very hard to find them.'

'I'm into Smurfs,' I began. 'You know, those shitty little gnomes from when we were kids. The blue ones. I've already got one thousand, four hundred and eighty-three. Counting this one, one thousand, four hundred and eighty-four. I think it's nostalgia. Nostalgia makes people do strange things. I've got friends who suddenly start dancing in an enthusiastic frenzy to the songs they loathed when they were young, and I collect Smurfs. Oh, man, you'd never believe how many Smurfs they actually produced. For almost every kind of person there is, they produced the Smurf equivalent. To be honest, I'm thinking of one day publishing a scientific treatise on the Smurf phenomenon, I really am. My thesis is that the Smurf is the best reflection of the 1970s. Female emancipation, for instance, or the technology that suddenly became available to the general public, you see it all reflected in Smurfs. Once you think it through. You've actually brought up something important, Frankie. There are bricklayer Smurfs, alcoholic Smurfs, Indian Smurfs, nurse Smurfs, singer Smurfs, hairy Smurfs, you name it. But what I've just realized, *ka-boom*, all of a sudden: I don't know of a single example of a Jew Smurf. Do you think it even exists, the Jew Smurf? You know, one with earlocks sticking out under its hat? I know of Negro Smurfs, I've got three of them. But Jew Smurfs?'

But Frankie couldn't help me. Smurfs weren't his territory.

'I'm going to throw a party for Smurf number one thousand five hundred.'

I was overdoing it, I knew it, I'd even shocked myself by crapping on so ardently about Smurfs – the things I was capable of. I'd even run the risk of being believed. If I'd achieved anything with my blathering rant, it was that Frankie got sick of the subject of collecting and suddenly changed tack.

'It's actually quite a coincidence bumping into you like this. Just last week I thought of you, at the Arsendegem cemetery. I walked past your father's grave and thought, oh yeah, that's right, I'd forgotten that guy even existed, I wonder how his son's doing.'

That's another reason I hate conversations: they can be about Smurfs one minute and the next you're talking about your father's headstone.

My father's grave, I greet it sometimes driving past. As the Arsendegem cemetery lies next to the motorway I take to the coast, I see the walls of his boneyard from behind the wheel. I nod briefly, despite finding it a bit silly, and greet him in my thoughts. Hey, Dad, it's me again, lots of traffic. I'm on my way here or there and my sweetheart is with me again. It's a shame you never laid eyes on her, she's a beautiful girl. Things like that. It means that I never get to see the sea any more without thinking of my father. The sea, the same sea he once stared at through a difficult night on the pier, thinking of his death – old news now – wavering as to whether it would be the sea in which he would take his own life. But my father was a swimmer: in more merciful years he had been grateful to the water that lifted him up as he did his relaxed backstroke through the North Sea; he would have been betraying that same water if he had chosen an undoubtedly gruesome death by drowning that night. That was why he returned home by train the following morning without any seaweed in his lungs, without mussels on his back, to add the finishing touch to our breakfast table with the words, 'I couldn't do it.' The sea is the grave I would have preferred for him, you shouldn't bury a drinker on dry land, and I'm deeply sorry that, when his familiar smile found its final, incomprehensibly silent home on a death mask, we didn't scatter his ashes over those vast waters while a foghorn played *Kaddish*. Now he's lying there, even though it makes no difference to him, in wind-blasted Arsendegem. Without even a bottomless amphora at his feet so that, in keeping with Hellenic custom, people could pour in a bottle of wine when appropriate to succour the dead. Soon I can expect another absurd letter from the Arsendegem town council informing me that the lease for my father's last resting place is about to expire and enquiring whether I wish to extend said lease for however many years and, if so, could I please transfer the correct amount to the correct account. They won't leave him in peace. It used to be the landlords of the dilapidated dumps we lived in who would throw him out on the street at the end of a cycle of demands and bailiffs, after which we'd move in with my grandmother. Soon the day will come when he'll be thrown out of his own grave as a chronic defaulter.

'Do you ever get back to Arsendegem?' Frankie asked.

I don't keep precise records, but I must visit my father's grave about once every five years. I can't see any direct reason for these visits, unless I don't want to see it. It's something that's just suddenly there, a pointless desire to go to the cemetery. And then I stand there, neither closer nor further away from him than if I was at home sitting on the sofa, but still, I'm there and he is too, somehow. That's what I tell myself in those moments, otherwise there's no point to it at all. I don't know how long I stand there. I don't believe I've ever stood there mourning faithfully in a downpour, but statistically speaking it must have been spitting now and then, there must have been a bit of drizzle at least once or twice. I always light up a cigarette at his grave, and going by the number of butts at the cemetery, I'm not the only one. It's surprising how few empty bottles you find there. Odd that it's never occurred to me to get drunk there, but that I always wait until I've left the cemetery before letting my stations of the cross lead me into all the pubs where, in my thoughts, I still see him leaning on the bar in the middle of one of his many retellings to someone who's half asleep. That cigarette. I light it up. That's what I start with. A ritual, my toxic prayer made up of nitrosamines, formaldehyde, nicotine and benzene. And then I let my gaze glide over the cemetery, which has expanded a little more with every visit, and where there's always a woman down on her hands and knees with a bucket and a sponge to wash the grave-stone of her deceased hubby, because in towns like this letting your bloke rot away under a dirty stone is still the sign of a bad wife. I feel those scrubbing frumps look up from their sponges and I feel them thinking: Well, I'll be, if it's not young Verhulst. He still comes to see his dad sometimes. If I raise a hand they feel caught out and start rubbing the marble even harder. The next day my name will do the rounds: They've seen me. Young Verhulst has been spotted back in Arsendegem again, puffing away in the afternoon at Mad P.'s grave, and glassy-eyed that evening at the bar of the Social. It's only when I've assured myself that I'm alone with my father which, given the circum-stances, amounts to being alone by myself, that I speak, out loud: 'Dad, it's time to get up.' Because that's the only sentence I know whose effect won't disillusion me, it's the sentence I said so often standing beside him. It's time to get up, and he stayed lying there, pissed out of his skull, still in bed at that stage. I never left the Arsendegem cemetery cheated, but always thinking: If he's too late for work it's his own fault. I tried to get him up out of bed but he refused again. He can kiss my arse. That's enough to keep me going for another five years.

But to get back to the matter in hand, I answered Frankie's question with, 'Ah, now and then.'

On the rare occasions I head back to Arsendegem – the Prodigal Son, the Good Son, a Son no matter what – I go from pub to pub knowing I won't need to visit three before finding my uncles in a predictable state at the bar, in their regular spots that nobody else dares occupy, as if their names have been written on the barstools with the blood of a transgressor. Then I enjoy the look our Girder tosses me like a bunch of flowers from behind his three half-full glasses, a gleaming gaze, eyes that, in moments like this, don't even need the booze to look as wet as a fried egg that's been taken off the gas too soon. Our Herman has eyes like that too: they must have disarmed many a woman when he staggered home late in a terrible state. Girder will invariably call me his little brother – and there's not much that can make me happier than having this villainous pig call me his little brother – and then we hug and kiss each other, although we've never been big kissers. And then we drink. The first five beers go down in no time. The first to let the amber fluid fuddle him is our Herman, overcome by the unexpected memories I've evoked of his dead brother, and he will raise his voice to the fossils around him, calling out, 'Hey, everybody, do you remember this guy?' Playing it safe at the same time by immediately providing the answer. 'This is Dimitri, our P.'s son.' The older ones are visibly surprised. They randomize the flabby disc of their increasingly crippled memory and see, in the best instance, a distant flash of my face as a child. 'Little Dimmy ... Oh yeah, I know him well. I remember him asleep here on the pool table as a kid. I used to go whoring with his dad. He was a barrel of laughs, his dad, one of a kind. Bloody old P., how long's he been pushing 'em up now?' The younger ones didn't even look up. They weren't going to break their concentration on the pinball machine for the sudden arrival of the stranger I am to them, already annoyed about somebody else getting all the attention just because of his presence. In my thoughts I give them a soundtrack, a crackling, scratched single of Roberta Flack singing, 'Sad young men are growing old.' Played on a jukebox, but by accident, because someone typed in the wrong number. They're the new generation and I realize that I've swindled fate by not being the one standing there with his beer on the pinball machine. These guys have taken my place, may they never realize it. The pigs are getting old: it is rarer and rarer that my uncles are challenged to a drinking race, and they are no longer seen as worthy opposition in the arm-wrestling matches that determine the participants' share of the town's available crumpet, making or breaking the reputations they are so desperate to retain.

That was the Arsendegem I returned to every now and then, but there wasn't the faintest possibility of Frankie knowing that town, even if he still lived there and saw my uncles more often than I did, as shadows wandering the streets, as losers, cockroaches. The misfortunate have a more realistic view of the world; my love for my uncles is vast and incomprehensible, but no one has ever had the gall to demand comprehensibility of love. Frankie must have felt that he had to weigh his words carefully. He didn't even come close to mentioning my uncles, and talked about an Arsendegem I've never known, a place I feel doesn't even exist. Frankie told me about the diploma he'd obtained, the job he did, his wife, the children that justified her existence, the house that was probably built around the TV. I know, they just happen to be the kind of facts people exchange when seeing each other again after a long time, the essence of existence, the themes that always determine the cut and thrust of old friends' chit-chat. But still . . . I sometimes find the essence of existence extremely tedious. I had to go. He thought it was a true pleasure to have seen me again, no doubt, and gave me the card with the address that I later copied into my new address book, and later still tore out of my address book, immediately losing all contact with people whose name began with T. T for Tienpont, Frankie Tienpont. Blunders are for making; I gave him my number in return.

His telephone voice was ugly too. It was about three months after our superfluous encounter that he rang to ask if I wanted to drop by sometime. I didn't. 'When?' I asked. 'Whenever suits you,' he said. It didn't suit me. It would never suit me. The following Sunday I was sitting in an armchair in his living room, kidding myself that I was using his invitation as an excuse to go back to Arsendegem, camouflage for the great longing I sometimes feel for the things that are past – a lie and a sign of a geriatric soul.

Frankie's house looked just like I'd imagined it. He was home alone and I got the impression that wasn't going to change much in the near future. Although he'd told me about his children in Chiny, there was nothing to suggest that any children had been here recently. Children are like pets, you can smell their presence. I had every reason in the world to assume that Frankie's wife – there weren't any photos of her anywhere, not on a cupboard and not pinned to the wallpaper – had left him and taken the kids with her. The longer I sat there in Frankie's tasteless leather armchair, the more certain I became: this boyo's been dumped. His wife had done the deed with someone else, felt love for the first time after five years of marriage and found the courage to listen to her heart. And Frankie, who had kept his loneliness gagged all that time by occupying himself with wife and child and the bacon he had to bring home, must suddenly have realized how alone he was, how alone he had been all these years, and had now fallen back on the few people he had once known. I didn't ask him about his kids and missus, the signs were there, I knew them well. Only the lonely, dum, dum, dum, dooby doo-wah.

'So,' I asked, 'what's up?'

'What do you mean?'

'What did you ask me to drop by for? There must be some reason.

At least, there are some people who need a reason for something like that, and you strike me as one of them.'

'Oh, nothing special. I thought it was nice bumping into you and I thought: why not make up for lost time?'

The word alone: 'nice'.

'Okay,' I said.

A bowl of crisps on the coffee table remained untouched. I enjoyed watching him do his best to come up with subjects of conversation that might draw me in. His face had started to look like his father's, the face of the man who forbade his son from associating with a Verhulst. Frankie blathered on for quite a while, I've forgotten which subjects he raised in his fruitless attempt, I left him to it, annoyed in the meantime by a buzzing I recognized but couldn't place. Was it the floor heating? The motor of an oil-fuelled boiler that was still pumping warmth through the bricks of this ghost house?

'My wife's left me,' Frankie said suddenly, probably because his supply of blah-blah had run dry.

'I know,' I said unaffected, amused even.

'What do you mean, you know? How do you know?'

'I know. That's what counts.'

'Did your uncles tell you?'

What would my uncles be doing telling me that the wife of a twerp like Frankie had scarpered? His family couldn't possibly fall into their fields of interest.

'There's something I have to tell you,' he began.

The buzzing was getting on my nerves.

'My wife, she . . .'

'. . . fucked someone else? These things happen, Frankie. I'm not a good counsellor in that area.'

'She went to bed with your Uncle Heavy.'

Well, well, well, what a brilliant story. Frankie's missus had gone for a roll with a Verhulst. My uncles truly were the guardians of justice.

'I guess that kind of makes us family,' I said to rub it in.

He poured himself a whisky. A scene from *Dallas*.

'She's gone. My wife's gone. I hit her when she told me. I know it was wrong, but I couldn't help myself. Right in the face with the kids watching and now she's gone. It's been almost four weeks and I haven't heard a word. She took the kids. I don't even know if they miss me. Can you tell me if my wife is still with your Heavy?'

'It's none of my business, Frankie, it's your problem. I'm staying out of it.'

'I don't get it. My wife and your Heavy!'

'What don't you get about it, Frankie? Don't you understand your wife feeling good with a horrible Verhulst, her falling in love with a drunk from Kerkveld Road, her walking out on you for a bloody idiot who doesn't have a qualification to his name, unemployed and such bad manners that he eats with his elbows on the table? Is that what you don't get, Frankie?'

He seemed to understand what I was working up to and didn't reply.

'Is that why you asked me to drop by?'

He nodded. I should have asked for petrol money.

'To be frank, Frankie, I think what's happened to you is fabulous. It's almost enough to make me religious. This wrath is so fitting, it's fantastic. You had it coming.'

'Your Heavy is ten years older than my wife.'

'I'm not interested, Frankie, honestly. It's your problem. I really don't give a fuck, so just shut up about it.'

'But can you please just tell me if my wife is still at your Heavy's? That's all I'm asking. I'm desperate.'

'Frankie, get it into that thick head of yours. For the last time, work it out yourself.'

I must have sounded absolutely determined because he finally shut his trap and stared into space as pathetically as only a man whose wife has left him can. How often had I seen a man sitting in an armchair with his legs wide, his elbows resting on his knees, and his forehead supported by his hands? His eyes brimmed as he tried to get a grip on himself, but I knew he wouldn't succeed. A few more minutes and the tears would be leaving their snail trails down his cheeks. He'd start sobbing, then blubbing, for a good five minutes, until he finally apologized for acting like a baby and went off to wash his face at the sink. His life was fucked. Everything he'd built up had collapsed around him. An everyday occurrence, fate is always flaring up somewhere, but usually more blindly than in this delectable instance. I sat in his armchair, listened to him howl and watched his muscles spasm as he started making the moronic movements that would have been put down to hysteria if he'd been a woman. I left him to it. It was the key scene in my own American soap opera. In the end, all that whimpering would give him a headache and he'd stop of his own accord.

'Frankie, can you tell me what that annoying sound is in your living room and then turn it off?'

He wiped away his tears with one of his children's handkerchiefs; there were pictures of Bambi on it. 'What did you say?'

'Can you kill the constant fucking drone? Maybe your wife left you to get away from that noise.'

'What noise?'

'What noise? The vrrr, vrrrr. I don't have to imitate it for you, do I? You can hear it yourself.'

'Oh, that. That's my trains.'

'Your trains? Those little trains from the old days? Do you still collect them?'

That's how simple people are: just a moment ago, forsaken by God and his wife, he sat juddering in his armchair, howling like a baby. And now he tastes the gratification of getting some attention, thanks to the model trains of his childhood, and slides his misery aside.

'I keep my trains running non-stop. I've built a complete railway network in the cellar, just like the old days but much bigger, and I have all my trains running on it. Would you like to see my collection?'

Of course I didn't want to see his collection. I wanted to go home.

'If it will make you happy, Frankie, then I'll have a quick look at your non-stop trains, okay?'

'You'll be shocked. My collection is nothing like it was the last time you saw it. But first I'll go and wash my face.'

While he got rid of his sissy tears, using cold water to bring his face back to the land of the living, I lit a cigarette. It was obvious that this was the kind of house where smoking was not allowed, a dwelling that had to smell constantly of the holy cleansing product, and because I couldn't find an ashtray anywhere I tipped my ash into a flowerpot. The flowers would wilt soon anyway, flowers can't be bothered surviving for just anyone. Puffing away, I walked through the house, studying the meagre contents of the CD rack and the bookcase with its twisted thematic classification and emphasis on World War II. I leafed through the Märklin model train catalogues on the coffee table, and sent my cigarette flying in a high arc over the terrace with a flick of my index finger.

'Sorry.' He returned from the bathroom. 'I lost it for a moment there. I've been acting like a baby. You must think I'm pathetic.'

I could only agree with him.

'Can I ask just one thing? Have you been smoking in here?'

'Don't get your knickers in a twist, Frankie, it's my armpits. It's a family ailment, all the Verhulsts suffer from it, just ask your father. Or your wife.'

I followed him to the cellar, the big kid, where I looked at his collection. The trains – I didn't count them, but there were a lot – ran up hill and down dale, weekdays and holidays, morning, noon and night, day in, day out, constantly. And now, too, those trains didn't crash into each other once. You'd have to be a mathematical monster to work out a schedule to keep this many trains chugging perfectly round your cellar. The miniature landscape was even more realistic than it had been in his childhood. And the little Jews he had started collecting as well were all propped together in the cattle wagons.

A Cured Man

They'd fattened him up. At first we thought it was just his haircut, which was a little too severe, but after a thorough inspection we had to discount all optical illusions and conclude that my father really had put on weight, about two stone by our estimate. Before making his long-awaited return that morning, he'd washed his hair with the best shampoo he could afford, given his almost Maghrebi moustache a proud, neat trim, and used brilliantine to shape his magnificent curls into the gentle waves of a restful sea. We had to hand it to him, he was a handsome man, the most handsome of all of us, even if he knew it. He had no trouble playing the part. Auntie Rosie had given him a fantastic and probably expensive tracksuit, a sky blue outfit that suited him down to the ground and which he was now wearing, out of gratitude, and to demonstrate how glad he was to have it. He exuded self-confidence, and if we were smart we'd stick close to him and try to breathe some of it in.

We hadn't hung up streamers and balloons, there was no cake in the fridge, and a bottle of champagne would have been pretty inappropriate, but we had arms we could open, so that he could fall into them and let us close them tightly around him. This was my father and I was proud of him, I admired him, I adored him. More than the most handsome of all of us, he was the most handsome man I had ever seen, a god in disguise. He'd completed his first three months in the drying-out clinic, he'd stuck it out, soon he'd sit down and tell us what it had been like. Now he was facing his first hard task: surviving two days and one night on the wagon in the reality he'd been hurled back into. Freedom. He had been looking forward to his freedom, unlike the recidivists who were terrified of their two days' leave. They begged to be allowed to stay at the clinic and would have sold their miserable forty-eight hours of liberty to the first comer to stay shackled to its strict regime. Not my father though, he was glad to finally see us again.

He put down his bag of dirty clothes. His socks, his underwear, his T-shirts. My grandmother didn't have to wash the things – after all, the clinic had a small laundrette where the patients could throw their own clothes in a drum – but she grabbed the bag gratefully, glad to be able to do something for her brave son. She was like that. As if for three months she had missed having to soak the clothes my father had shat in and vomited over in a bucket overnight before washing them by hand as her washing machine had proven inadequate for these specific cases. She tipped his clothes out of the bag in the middle of the kitchen and sorted them into piles according to washing programme, and it was plain that my father hadn't shat or pissed his pants once and that he had been taking excellent care of himself and had himself under control, as he claimed.

My uncles were still in bed, knackered from a Friday night on which they had needed to prove themselves, on which they had demanded their spot in the pecking order and laid their claim to all of the pubs' rights and women. They couldn't wait to sleep off their headaches, because soon it would be Saturday night, the queen of nights, and they would need to be ready to defend their reputation. My grandmother stood at the bottom of the stairs and called, a wolf to her cubs, 'Heavy, Herman, Girder, get up, our P. is here!' And it must be said that all three of them, despite their comatose states, immediately threw the sheets off their bodies and raced downstairs with their arms swinging childishly to be reunited with the biggest clown in the family.

'P., for fuck's sake, man, you've put on weight.'

See, everybody said so. The years in which he dutifully drank himself into serial oblivion had robbed him of his appetite. It had happened in phases. First he had no longer managed to get a bite down his throat in the morning. Smokers reach that phase too, and even if they one day succeed in quitting the habit, they continue to find breakfast the most difficult meal and probably skip it. But my father had moved on from that stage long ago – he couldn't bear to eat solid food at midday either. And when he ate, he stuffed his throat with the fatty products drunks use to combat hangovers, burdening their livers that little bit more: eggs, almost liquefied cheeses, overripe and stinking, sardines in oil, chips soaked in gravy. And before his body could absorb the nutritional value of the meal, he'd puked it up somewhere. We weren't inclined to beer guts, we were lucky in that, our build always tended to the emaciated, making us more susceptible to all kinds of cancers and leaving our trousers flapping around our legs long before it came back into fashion. And it would come back into fashion, nothing ugly stays away for ever. But there he sat, my dad, as grand as could be, as proud as a peacock, leaning on our round kitchen table with the eternal oilcloth our cigarettes had burned holes in, enjoying our gazes. 'Fucking hell, P., you've put on weight.'

He told us about the breakfast cereal he now spooned up out of a bowl of skimmed milk every morning. None of us had ever seen a breakfast cereal, even its existence had been unknown to us, but it sounded disgusting all the same. Breakfast bloody cereal, with bits of fresh bloody apple and the juice of two oranges. And yoghurt. Enough to shit a brick. And all of that at an hour at which he otherwise had a few beers under his belt, how did he manage it? He told us about the sports he practised there daily, football and cricket and softball and basketball and squash, and how his body had adjusted to so much exercise. He showed us his muscles, and it was true, my father would no longer be picked up and put down a few yards further away by a hard gust of wind. In the evening they played games, moronic but enjoyable, and in between he learned all kinds of skills that would come in handy in everyday life. But he had been through hell, especially at the start. Lucifer had flambéed all the food with whisky and cognac, the breath of every hellhound smelled of booze, and barman Beelzebub was constantly offering free rounds for all the backsliders. But he had stuck to it and here he was, home for two days. Tomorrow he had to check back in, 5 p.m. at the latest, and if he was found to be completely sober they would let him come home every weekend from now on. If not, he would have to keep to the clinic's strictest regime for another three months, without any further contact with the outside world. But he was ready, physically he'd already kicked the habit, he didn't even think about beer. And if he did think about it, it was as an arch enemy, a bitter cup to shun for evermore. His mother gleamed. All of a sudden she was in the running for happiest woman in the world and the young girls who were being kissed by the liar of their dreams at that same instant could only see her as tough competition.

At noon my father demonstrated his appetite over a plate of roast pork and unequalled cauliflower cheese. My uncles had already smoked their post-luncheon cigarettes all the way down to the filter, but he helped himself to more and more and more. All the time loudly describing the clinic and the magnificent arses of the female nursing staff. He had drawn courage from seeing other cases free themselves of their addictions. Compared with them he was, for want of a better expression, small beer. Junkies who have snorted away their nasal septum, who spread their testicles in search of a last decent vein, then shot up into it with dirty needles. Hysterical bitches who have plundered chemists and swallowed everything they could get their hands on. Cases like that. And they too had succeeded. If people like that could do it! He was serious. It had been three months since he'd touched his last glass and he was ready for a brand-new life. It cost him two pots of coffee and three-quarters of a pack of cigarettes to tell his story, and when he was finally finished he asked, 'How's things here?'

Hmm, how *were* things here? How *could* things here be? Like always, surely? It had been quieter without him, true.

'What's been happening the last three months?'

What always happened. My uncles could hardly start promoting the lifestyle my father was trying to renounce. They'd hit the bottle and chased women. When their money ran out, they'd accepted cash jobs on building sites until they had enough to start drinking again. Bailiffs had come calling, they'd spent some nights in the clink for an assault here and a battery there, they'd been cut off the dole again. Nothing special.

'And you?' He looked at me. 'How's school, killer?'

I showed him my school reports for the last three months. Red was the dominant colour.

'Did you do your best?'

I nodded.

'That's what matters. As long as you do your best, I'm happy.'

My uncles got thirsty and slipped out of the house, at least tactful enough to not invite my father to join them.

It must have hit my father like a smack in the gob when he put his stuff in our bedroom. The smell of alcohol, exhaled in my uncle's snores, must have come to him as a temptation. Tonight he would have to sleep in that smell and there was a fair chance of his being woken deeper into that night, towards dawn, and therefore actually in the shallowness of the day, from his potentially troubled sleep by his singing brothers and the much more troubling, inescapable impression that they were happier than him. He opened the windows silently. Anyone who thought my father would capitulate then and there, in the bedroom, realizing the hopelessness of his struggle, can be forgiven.

'Put on your shoes and some clean socks. I've got a surprise for you,' he said, as if he hadn't surprised me enough already. Half an hour later I was sitting next to him on a cheerless bus on a ripped seat the town's youth and future had decorated with spouting phalluses, next to a window on which they had written telephone numbers in the dust under the empty promise, 'I'll suck you off free.' Anyone who owned a car refused, understandably, to set foot on a bus. Our public transport was used exclusively by yapping schoolchildren, poor buggers, grandmothers on their way to the market and drunks who often fell asleep and missed the stop they thought they were supposed to get off at. I was familiar with every category of bus passenger. This time too there was a pisshead on the bus, and he did what pissheads who don't fall asleep are supposed to do to justify their status: he harassed a woman. She saw her doom approaching but tried to radiate confidence as he staggered from pole to pole before plonking himself down on the bench next to her. He threw his arm around her fear-paralysed neck. She was so beautiful. That was something he just had to tell her. And it would be a thousand times better to be married to her instead of the slut who'd left him for someone else. My father must have seen himself there. His *former* self: that explained the triumphant look in his eyes. Despite a libido that was undoubtedly shot to pieces, he too must have harassed many a girl, and it will always be my father who springs to mind when I'm taking the last subway home in a big city and see the almost obligatory drunk bringing his stinking breath too close to the face of a solitary girl. Maybe my father felt shame that afternoon, realizing that he had forced his completely shit-faced self on others all those years. Inasmuch as he could remember it. Only rarely did the women have the courage to humiliate the men and slap them in the face; even brawny bus drivers didn't always have the nerve to chuck troublemakers off the bus: they were content to get back to the depot in one piece and finally be allowed to go home.

The surprise this bus was carrying us to was located in Bloemkool Street, a grey artery that led to the centre of Aalst, right through the old neighbourhoods that didn't even need rain to look like a set for an Irish film. But that street was also home to Colmar, pretty much the dearest and best shop for sporting goods we knew and the place where my father had decided to let me pick out a pair of spikes. With the money he'd saved in three teetotal months, a good pair of running shoes suddenly belonged to the realm of possibility, and there would be enough left over to present my teeth to a dentist for once and to acquire a coat that was thick enough to make you long for a severe winter.

Spikes. It was true, I ran in those years, keen and determined, mostly long distance and preferably in the fields in the months of October and November, when the countryside smelled best and the seed heads were on the fescue grass. I was no great talent, but I was better than average, and now and then I'd come back from a race with a medal or even a trophy, let's say by accident, when the better runners slumped. Athletics was the obvious sport for the badly off – it didn't require any facilities at all. You could run anywhere, free of charge. Those were the years in which the great runner Zola Budd proved that you could even shatter records barefoot, and there was a whole generation of up-and-coming Ethiopians and Kenyans who would provide the final proof that poverty was better than a pair of spikes for aspiring long-distance runners, which didn't stop me from being delighted with my new footwear. The potential was there, and almost all of the preconditions for making me a decent runner today had been fulfilled. My stamina was good, very good actually, if I'm allowed to be so immodest, and it is without resentment that I observe that I couldn't knock off 5,000 metres today in less than half an hour. At least, I assume that's the case, because it's been a long time since I even thought about lumbering through lap after lap in a pair of shorts. The thought of even leaving the house in shorts is too much to bear, let alone having to start running in that get-up. It was only later, when I read Alan Sillitoe's best-known work, *The Loneliness of the Long Distance Runner*, that I realized that it had been pure logic that had turned me into a runner as a child. Running was the sport of the boarding schools, orphanages, borstals and boys' homes that were my destiny. Schools were proud of their students' sporting exploits and only too fond of linking their name and reputation to a winner, as if their discipline and musty teaching methods had helped create him. No wonder I invariably failed at interschool meetings. Like the main character in the novella, I loathed the prospect of scoring a victor's trophy for my school.

And besides all that, running was the sport I'd inherited from my father. I knew that in his younger years he had acquitted himself well in this area and I remember the story from my earliest childhood about our gas cooker being the first prize my father won in a cross-country race. My mother was in raptures and imagined a whole house furnished by my father's leg power. Many times I had to listen to how he was trained by his own father who, cigar in mouth, pursued him along the entire practice route by moped. Hence my father's joy when I joined the athletics club. Hence the pleasure with which he gave me a pair of very pricey spikes. The vanity of having his son follow in his footsteps.

'You'd better wear those shoes in before you show up at a race with 'em.'

That same afternoon, my father had me in my training kit out on a field where the maize shot up so high in summer that Arsendegem's lucky young things went there to fuck, even if that's undoubtedly a chapter in the story of every town and village with maize fields. Keeping up a light jog alongside each other. 'Breathe every fourth step!' I thought he was daft, a typical thirty-something panicking about his age and overdoing things in an attempt to make up for lost time and recover muscle strength that was gone for ever. Gyms everywhere make a fortune from men like that. He might have stopped drinking, but he could never undo the damage he'd done to himself, and anyway, he was still a chain smoker who was now trying to kick the phlegm up out of lungs with his legs. He kept it up though – one, two, three, four and breathe, one, two, three, four and breathe – and gradually raised the tempo so that I had trouble keeping up with him. The struggle we were caught up in was the one fathers and sons never let rest until age decides it for ever, the struggle to prove who's strongest. Fathers keep handing their sons the patricidal weapon, begging to be defeated. The day was coming. I wouldn't need to be challenged to many more playful wrestling bouts before I would prove myself stronger than my father, leaving him behind with the proud knowledge that his offspring had reached physical maturity, but also with the painful realization that his decline had begun. But not yet. For now, my father ran faster, and especially further; my spleen was about to burst when I asked him to take it a bit easier. And his relief at hearing my words was clear: he was knackered too, over the last thousand metres his willpower had taken over from his legs.

'You're a bloody good runner, lad,' he panted. He looked pale, but I could have been looking paler.

'Them spikes fit right?'

Nothing had ever fitted as well as the running shoes on my feet.

'You racing tomorrow?'

I nodded. I must have nodded a lot in those days.

'I'll be there to watch.'

The phenomenon of parental supporters was known to me, I heard them every week calling out their sons' names from the sidelines, mostly preceded by an uninspired 'Go', and occasionally followed by a piece of tactical advice that didn't make any sense. Most annoying were the fathers who rode their bikes alongside the course. It was something I could definitely do without. Although I was never able to convince a juvenile-court judge as much, I already felt that I had a father who was interested in me. Having him attend my races wasn't going to strengthen that feeling, and if I hadn't had it, it wouldn't have evoked it. But I could understand my father wanting to show that he was a father, for himself more than anything. Plus he had just spent three months in a drying-out clinic and it was quite conceivable that he had missed both his son and fatherhood. Having my father cheer me on the next day would only make me feel like I had to end up in the top three at least. I'd heard so many stories about expectations by then that I knew what they meant. Oh well, if he was so keen on coming to watch me run, I'd just have to let him.

Although no one would have blamed him for doing so, my father didn't lie down on the sofa to rest after our training session, weary but satisfied. Instead he strode restlessly around the house until he had found something to do. The discovery of an old tin of varnish calmed him down for a while. He pounced enthusiastically on the shed door, which didn't really need renovating, and gave it a new coat of varnish. And because varnishing a shed door doesn't take hours, not even for a clumsy perfectionist, he immediately grabbed the lawnmower afterwards and cut our very small lawn, although that too was completely futile. There will never be enough shed doors and lawns in the world to give an ex-drinker the peace of mind he'd find in a crate of beer.

Biting his nails, he bore the vacuousness of television. He lit one cigarette off the other, tugged his moustache, fidgeted constantly with his toes and drank coffee after coffee. Finally he was able to vent his nervousness on an evening meal of seven slices of bread with bacon and a thick slathering of mustard. He dragged himself from one bloated meal to the next, chewing up biros and toothpicks. In this state he could have serviced a dozen exceptionally fit women, but would have driven them, too, to complete exhaustion before discovering that they didn't still the right hunger. Our Girder asked him about it when he came back home for tea, something he did to get himself ready for the serious drinking that would come later that evening.

'Three months in a clinic – man, I bet you've got blisters on your fingers from wanking so much.'

'Your eyes would pop out that ugly head of yours if you knew who's getting into each other's pants there. Staff with staff, clients with clients, staff with clients.'

'You serious? Come on, if it's like that I'll check in too. That way anyone could get off the booze.'

'So you think. I'd like to see you go without.'

By this time our Herman had shown up too – judging by the angle of his eyes, his day was already twenty beers old – and asked my father if he was coming to the pub with them later.

'You have to show your mug there, lad. Everybody thinks you're a loon 'cause you've already spent three months in the nuthouse. People say, "Your P.'s mad." I'm sick of hearing them say you're mad, cause then I have to smash the buggers' faces in and I'm not always in the mood for it. Please, just put in an appearance so they can see you're still normal.'

'Yeah, P.,' Girder said. 'People keep asking about you the whole time. They miss you. Everyone'll be there, it's pool night. Willy the Postman, Fonske, Peter Stocking, Skinny André, Fatso Swa, the lisping curate, Rudy and Arlette, Jean-Paul Cannoot, Freddy the barber, Kamiel from Mael . . . They're all there waiting for you.'

'And just because you go to the pub doesn't mean you have to drink,' Herman offered in an attempt at diplomacy. 'They sell Tourtel there too.'

Tourtel was the first brand of non-alcoholic beer we'd ever heard of and we looked down on it from a great height. Cultural pessimism is the term that best approaches what we felt when Tourtel came onto the market, and we saw comparable forms of impoverishment taking hold all through society: the shelves of the shops suddenly contained packets of decaffeinated coffee, which we refused to purchase; chemists with a biased take on well-being shamelessly promoted nicotine-free cigarettes; and butter without a trace of fat made mothers more modern. We blamed it on the Americans, who forced their barbarism on the rest of the world by inventing all kinds of products that were unfit for human consumption.

'Next thing they'll come up with meat-free meat,' said our Herman. He always exaggerated.

Tourtel was something my father had his own ideas about: non-alcoholic beer was to real beer what a sex-doll was to a real woman, and just because he'd quit drinking he wasn't going to modify that opinion. He'd rather spend the whole night guzzling little glasses of water.

'Fine, drink your little glasses of water all night, what do we care? What you going to do? Sit here on the sofa all night watching German TV with Mum? Don't be daft. Come and have a game of pool!'

My father couldn't avoid alcohol for the rest of his life, he knew that as well as anyone. At some stage he'd have to go back to work and start delivering letters again. No other postman had as many pubs on his route as my father, he'd counted himself lucky on that score. The Geraardsbergen Gate, Lange Zout Street, Korte Zout Street, the market square. That's where the sleaziest pubs were, where the human fauna slithered in at night, and all the landladies knew their duty and poured the postman a drink when he dropped the letters and newspapers on the bar. In the winter, offering the postman a shot of something to fortify him against the freezing temperatures and the vicious wind was a universally accepted act of charity. Port, for instance. The stronger the drink, the more they played it down. A tiny little nip of cognac, perhaps? To a postman's liver, spring seemed impossibly distant, and that estimation proved accurate for all too many of them. And when he arrived to hand some old bloke his pension, he definitely had to sit down at the kitchen table, where a bottle of jenever and two glasses would be waiting next to a box of cheap cigars decorated with a picture of a French king in nylon stockings. Tomorrow or the day after, a doctor would officially declare my father sober and wish him luck and then he would have to say no to all those jenevers and beers and ports on his round. No, no, no. With 'thank you' tacked on afterwards, because you have to stay polite when someone has just offered you a glass of downfall. How could he be capable of that if he wasn't even able to play a game of pool at the Social?

'You're right, I'll come and have a game of pool! But not to all hours.'

Through this whole conversation, my silent grandmother had picked imaginary fluff off her apron. She always did that when she was nervous, and it was a tick we might have adopted as well if we hadn't had moustaches to tug in difficult moments. 'Pierre, you're not going to be silly now?'

'I'm going to be sensible, Mum. There's nothing to worry about. Just a bit of pool with me mates and then back home. Really, I'll be back so fast you won't even know I'm gone.'

'But . . .'

'But what, Mum?'

'Never mind.'

He'd already had a bath. He'd have had five baths if it had switched his thoughts to nought. All he had to do now was pull on his coat and follow his brothers. Before slamming the door behind him, he turned back once, to look at me.

'Remember, killer, I'll be there tomorrow to watch the race. Get to bed early so you're nice and fit.'

I spent the rest of the evening with my grandmother, watching German TV shows. She was crazy about them but they always left her in a melancholy mood, presumably because those schmaltzy songs plunged her into a pool of contradictory feelings, taking her back to a war that had raged most furiously in her stomach, her years of hunger, but also to a youth that had taken place during an air-raid alert, in which people had danced and made love despite it all. By the time the country was liberated, my grandmother was already changing nappies, waiting at home for a man whose true face was already prematurely aged from the booze and who would impregnate her much too often while pissed as a newt. The most beautiful moments of her life must have taken place on the darkest pages of history, her happiness was overshadowed by the historians' gloomy black ink, and the progression from lean to fat years passed her by. When she sang along to those German oompah songs, a small smile curled her lips while she patted the tears from her eyes with a handkerchief she kept in the sleeve of her cardigan for just such an occasion. All those brass bands, tables full of hip-swinging fans, huntsmen's hats with pheasant feathers, knickerbockers held up by braces and yodelling Johannas had an effect on my grandmother that today's generation of quacks would probably put down to 'regenerative hypnosis', and I happily took on the role of listening ear on those Saturday evenings, enjoying her memories of Charlestons and the golden decade of the silver screen, when they went to the pictures instead of the cinema and a bare knee was an outrageous erogenous zone. She sat there in her easy chair, my shrunken grey angel, humming along to 'Johnny, wenn du Geburtstag hast'. Humming, because singing would have made me realize how sad she was. Stories were the harvest of her life, and now that I too am made up of more and more past, I have learnt to accept that in myself. Maybe, as a heathen, I should be less satisfied with this rather paltry profit margin on a whole existence, but my girl has already been obliged to interrupt my stories because she's heard them ten times or more. We too are dragging ourselves to an easy chair to tell stories from: we will become each other's story and one of us will have to tell it, and it's possible that I assume a little too fiercely that she'll be the one who has the last word. It could also be me who, on an evening I didn't want to make it to alone, sees that I am boring others with the happiness we have today and silences the sentences I have been hoarding for so long.

People can say what they like about German TV shows, but they're invariably upbeat and make the viewers feel like life is one big party. That makes the blow all the harder when you are thrown back into what you've temporarily forgotten when the host announces during the final credits that it's all over for tonight and the next episode of beer and song will be recorded in Westphalia or Munich or some-where else where they have a big October Hall at their disposal. My father hadn't come home yet and we knew that our clock was never a second fast or slow. Pool could take a long time. We watched a film that featured underlit breasts and mating women panting too close to the microphone – all within the bounds of the morally acceptable, but pleasantly entertaining for a boy – in which the characters were destined to have children and marital arguments; fatal diseases were okay too, as long as the story line rushed towards a depressing end you could cobble a comforting postscript on to – for instance, the terminal mother finds a respectable foster family for her children, or the adul-terous husband suffers a catastrophe no one begrudges him.

All of the actresses on all of the channels were finished panting, they were fully dressed again and the sweat on their skin had grown cold, and still my father hadn't come home. The films we could watch now weren't intended for my age group, the lighting was better, and I wasn't sure that my grandmother would have watched them even without me. She headed off to the bathroom, coughed up her dentures and pulled on a nightie. Then she pulled out all the electric plugs in case there was a lightning storm, because the forecast hadn't predicted any lightning storms and it was often wrong. Like every other night, I carried her bucket upstairs for her.

Pool could take a long time.

Like me, peering sideways from my bed, and my grandmother doing the same thing at that same time no doubt, my stupid mother must have spent many a night looking at the alarm clock. Getting her hopes up every time she heard a car slow down, thinking that it might be a taxi dropping off my dad, it no longer mattered what kind of state he was in, as long as he finally came home. Every rustling of a leaf under the window was an opportunity for her to convince herself that it was him, sliding a hand into a pocket to rummage for his keys. Only to fall asleep without realizing it, without clearly remembering the last hour she had read, semi-conscious, on the clock, and waking up in a room no one else had entered that night.

My father wasn't home when we had breakfast. And he wasn't home at dinnertime when my grandmother kept the green beans warm in case he showed up. My uncles weren't either, but they hadn't expressly stated that we could expect them. And that afternoon I ran my race with brand-new spikes without the pressure of a paternal supporter on my shoulders.

The Succession is Secured

There are two people I hate, I thought at the main entrance to the hospital. Two women. One gave birth to me and the other was giving birth to my child. You could see the two as interconnected in some ways, but pinning it down was difficult. The mind gets hazy when you're on the verge of suddenly changing from a son to a father. I would take a more considered view later, that's what laters are for. Everyone has their own character, their own ugly traits and features; ascertaining that there were some types I couldn't live with was my responsibility. I should have been more sensible. It's regrettable that I had to make a baby before acquiring these insights. It was also regrettable for the extremely expectant mother who, regardless of the situation, I would have to leave sooner or later if I had the courage to ever be happy. You're always a bit of an arsehole if you run out on a woman with a child, but it's because you weren't nearly a big enough arsehole to leave that woman before putting her up the stick. I'd done another great job there. I would make someone unhappy, or at least unhappier than she already was, or wanted to be, because some people seem to aspire to that: unhappiness as the path of least resistance.

A child as a going-away present – some women get less.

'Are we all right, there?' A hideous-looking nurse had spotted the disgust on my face but taken it for nausea. I was well on my way to hating the whole world. As if I cared, the world must have asked for it. It was that kind of day. Anyway, did I look like the kind of person you needed to ask if he was all right? I'm not squeamish. Even if her guts came squishing out, I wouldn't flinch.

'I'm just going for a little walk,' I said. 'Get rid of the cobwebs.'

At the same time I thought how stupid the expression was. What cobwebs?

'Your wife is dilated by however many centimetres. If I were you I wouldn't make that walk too long, not if you don't want to miss the birth.'

'She's not my wife, we're not married. Is there a cigarette machine here somewhere?'

'Excuse me, this is a hospital. You think we're going to hang cigarette machines up around the place?'

Twat. Cow. There were Coke machines in the corridors. If that wasn't poison, what was?

Fortunately I spotted a cancer patient at the main entrance. They usually have smokes on them.

There was a shop somewhere inside this cruddy building, specializing in newspapers and magazines. And medical romance novels. And flowers. And baskets of fumigated grapes. If I wasn't mistaken they had cigarettes there too. But it was still night time. Or at least, the summer sun had only just started its daily grind on a day that promised to be way too hot, and the shop's metal shutters were still down. I cadged a cigarette off the cancer patient.

'They're cruel here,' I said to have something to say. 'You can't light up a fag anywhere in the whole building. In hospitals you used to at least have separate smoking rooms. It stank to high heaven, but at least you didn't need to go outside for a puff on a cigarette. Smokers get treated more and more like lepers these days.'

'Is your wife in labour here?' he asked, instead of continuing the predictable conversation I had started up.

'She's not my wife!'

That more or less answered his question.

'Seventeen years ago I was standing here too, just like you are now, smoking until it was time for my wife to be induced. It ended up a caesarean.'

'Oh,' I said. What else was there to say? As if I gave a shit about his wife's caesarean.

That was how things went. The cycle of life. In a few years it would be my turn to take his place.

I was glad when he'd finished his cigarette and gone back to his room. 'See you later,' I said, although we both knew better. There I was. I'd never had the pleasure of meeting someone who hated children more than I did myself. My loathing for babies was so great that I had become persona non grata to female friends who had already reproduced themselves in the form of little creatures you couldn't say a bad word about: bright for their age, already talking really well for their age, little Einsteins no less. Nobody had ever made more of a fuss about not wanting any kids, yet here I stood while a stone's throw away someone was going through the usual pains to squeeze out a child, my child. I couldn't have cut a more ridiculous figure. How could I have been so sure, for all those years, that my fertility would adjust itself to my convictions, that the unwillingness in my brain would metastasize in my testicles? A character like me could only have been devised by Greek tragedians or by the scriptwriters of the kind of soap operas that put the logic of character development on the back burner in favour of general stupidity. There was still a very slim chance of the child being stillborn or coming out sufficiently deformed, as a chimaera if necessary, to be deemed non-viable. In that case I would find it difficult to conceal my delight. Even if I'd believed in God, it was hardly likely He'd have listened to a prayer for a – please, please – stillborn baby. The most wonderful thing that could happen to me was that the nurses would shortly treat me to pitying glances while laying a little mulatto in my arms. Then I wouldn't even need to explain why I was packing my bags. Everyone would feel sorry for me and support me even though the circumstances would be almost the same. To have been cheated on – had anyone ever wished for it as fervently as I did then?

I'd smoked my cigarette down to the filter, it tasted terrible, but I immediately craved another. Any other man in my shoes would have gone into the building to help his partner in what she would remember as either the most beautiful or the most painful moment of her life, maybe both. Not me. I couldn't. Maybe later. For the time being I was able to convince myself that there was nowhere better for me to be than at the main entrance of the hospital.

See, I thought, there's nothing outrageous about not wanting children. Our children are born in hospitals. They're a sickness. Wanting them is sicker.

A dog growled somewhere nearby but out of sight. Although the years that had passed made my suspicions absurd, I immediately thought of Blondi. Every time I heard a fierce dog, I thought of Blondi and the certainty of her revenge on Girder and me. A dog's life and maybe two had passed since her chain had been cut. An animal like that keeps her memory in her nose: if she needed to, she'd sniff her way round the globe till she found us, but find us she would. Vengefulness can extend a life, there were bound to be legendary examples of that. The voice of reason should have confronted me with the naked facts to bring me back into line, but what were the facts? We'd drowned Blondi's puppies. With pain in our hearts, but the dog didn't know that, and if she knew it, she ignored our innocence. What better revenge could Blondi have exacted than staying alive until I had a puppy of my own? Had any of us seen the bitch after she was set free? No. Had we seen her dead? No. Conclusion?

The growling of the dog came closer, a sound postmen have learned to take very seriously.

'Heel, I said! Heel! And fast! Sit! Sit! And stay sitting!'

The voice of someone who would never be offered a job as a telephonist – he should see that as an advantage. His dog, a male, had got agitated by the sight of another male, and he'd immediately grabbed it by the collar. And when I felt a pang of disillusion I immediately realized how idiotic it was to hope that an old dog from twenty years ago might plant her stinking fangs in a baby's soft throat. My baby's. I might have been willing to accept that fairy tales existed, but that didn't mean I was living one.

I checked my watch, an annoying tic I'd picked up from non-smokers. Maybe my child had already been born in the middle of that concrete colossus, or a nurse was in there running around like a mad cow looking for me so that I wouldn't miss the moment supreme. Another hour and the shop with cigarettes would be open.

A man had wandered out and you could tell from his alien grin that he had just become a father. The upstairs corridors were filling with grinning men and soon they'd expect me to walk down those corridors with a grin on my face too. My entire immediate future filled with grinning men. In a few days I would see them at the Register Office at the town hall, where I would be one of them, having gone in to register the child's birth. It would need a name too, like boats, hideous villas and hurricanes. The man, dressed up for the occasion, pulled a telephone out of the pocket of his jacket and shouted, 'Good morning, Grandma, Grandpa, sorry for waking you up so earl . . .' Because that was something the two people on the other end of the line had just become, Grandma and Grandpa, that was obvious. 'A son,' he shouted, 'a son!' And I started to worry that shouting and saying everything twice might be symptoms of fatherhood.

I wouldn't ring anyone. My mother, at least if she was still alive, would wake up somewhere, I didn't know where, not realizing that she had just become a grandparent. I couldn't exclude the possibility of that happening to me one day too, because I would have to accept the whole crappy package. I too could now become a grandfather, even if that was thinking very far ahead. And my father? Would he have got pissed with a smile on his face today for the reason I reluctantly gave him? Would he have shown a little understanding?

('What? The kid's not wanted? An accident? You stupid shit, accidents don't happen any more with all the pills and johnnies and abortions you get these days. I know what an accident is, but you don't. When your mother fell pregnant with you, it was a terrible accident, my life was bloody fucked, but I didn't stand there in the maternity hospital with a face as long as yours.')

I know the story. It was what you'd call a classic for the occasions when my parents sat around a table with other young couples. Apparently the birth of a child had made such an impression on them that they found it hard not to raise the subject. It was either that or dredging up sleazy jokes that made the women feel like they'd been reduced to the level of the hunk of meat now bleeding on their plate, next to a couple of potato croquettes that slurped up the excess juices and tasted like soaked newspaper, my mother's culinary speciality that we all praised and would continue to praise until the day we were forced to poke our forks into other pots.

It was already the third or fourth time my mother had checked in with the nuns who were supposed to help me be born, and each time she had been sent home again because the sisters couldn't stick three fingers, let alone their whole fist, into her. In other words, there was no question at all of an alarming degree of dilation. Besides being something of a hypochondriac, she was also scared of pain, a combination you encounter often and one that I too am sometimes guilty of. On the other hand, I would like to leave a chink open for the possibility that my mother didn't entirely trust those nuns, and I wouldn't blame her for it at all. No woman alive should have an easy mind about giving birth in a Catholic maternity hospital, where jealous nuns can always give in to their sadistic tendencies the moment they get their paws on someone else's sin-drenched genitals, taking revenge for their own life of abstinence and prayer by using the forceps a little more often than strictly necessary. I have no trouble imagining a nun like that: she appears to me as a smirking hypocrite, five foot three tops, prising the pubic bones apart with a badly sterilized spreader, justifying her perversity with quotes from the Bible that describe labour pains as a necessary punishment, the fateful inheritance all women are condemned to, simply because the first woman on earth was a deceitful moron. So I do understand my mother's suspiciousness and the way she must have screamed blue murder every time she thought she was about to give birth to me.

The woman my father had very recently been forced to marry because of poorly controlled urges came back from the maternity hospital three or four times without a baby, and there can be no doubt that he ridiculed her for it. When she finally got her real labour pains on a Sunday afternoon full of cake and football results, he no longer believed her and she headed off to her torturers alone. When it was time she could call him at the pub, the Las Vegas, because we didn't have a phone. It made sense: he had to wait somewhere she could reach him.

It was a Monday morning and pouring outside when Sister Philomena's hands pulled me out of my mother by my head, not the best start imaginable. My father wasn't present and we were going to have to wait a long time for him to show up; that'd give me a chance to get used to waiting for him. He was sitting, as agreed, in the Las Vegas, the very pub where, approximately twenty-two weeks earlier, he had killed off his bachelor days – quick, quick – in a toilet. It was a little after ten when the phone rang in the Las Vegas and the early drinkers all called out to the landlord, 'Hey, Willy, if it's my wife tell her I'm not here.' A little after ten when Willy grabbed the receiver and asked, 'Come again, who?' After which he loudly called to my father, 'P.! It's for you! Maternity hospital!' And it must have gone quiet in the pub. They'd have pulled out the plug of the jukebox and stared at my father's eyes as he listened to the person on the other end of the line: blubby eyes that announced a birth to those who knew him. He hung up, took a brief deep breath to preserve his manliness and then relieved his friends of their curiosity. 'A son! I've got a son! Drinks all round!' And Willy took down his steins, glasses he brought back every year from Bavarian beer festivals, and filled them with beer, beer, beer. Beer for everyone. A man who'd just become a father had to get drunk to the gills. Tradition demanded it, and tradition was something you never refused.

He would definitely have taken my mother a bunch of flowers, if only the whole country hadn't been brought to a standstill on that of all days by striking civil servants *and* shopkeepers, one group presumably dissatisfied by their wages and the other by tax levels. Apart from a few pubs, no businesses were open at all, and neither buses nor taxis were running. The butchers let their chicken livers go off rather than sell them. And, of course, no florists were open anywhere. The flowering season was almost over: the butterfly bushes were bare, the sweetpeas and zinnias were finished, there was no goatsbeard left on the waterside and the last asters had been wiped out by the first autumn storm. That was why my father picked stinging nettles on the roadside, wrapped them elegantly in cling film and attached a beer mat as a card: 'For Mum.' He jumped on his post office bike with the bouquet of nettles in his postbag, hoping that the drizzle would sober him up a little. Did he sing on his bike? 'The Cherry Picker's Song'? 'The age of wonders lives on yet, the weather's dry and my cherry's wet.' Or 'The Ballad of the City Park Shitter'? 'It ain't easy to shit in the park, you can't always wait until dark. Without paper to wipe off your arse, use some leaves and maybe some grass . . .' and so on, for as many verses as it took him to get to the maternity hospital. He must have sung something. We always sang when we were happy. We sang when we drank till we were happy.

It's doubtful that Sister Philomena still regretted her earthly renunciation when she caught sight of my soaked father finally staggering down the corridor. Her platonic relationship with the Lord might not have hushed her itchings, but she probably still preferred it to the available men in our parts, who arrived drunk and with a bunch of stinging nettles for the woman who had borne them a child just hours before.

'You are?'

'Pierre Verhulst! My son was born here this morning. Can you tell me which ward my wife is in?'

She looked at the clock, a strange habit, really, for someone who believed in eternity, and said, 'I was thinking it must be a fatherless child. I'm afraid we've been seeing more and more of that around here the last few years.'

'Was the Holy Ghost on time when his little one was born, maybe?'

She peered at the nettles. 'Is that a bunch of flowers for your wife?'

'The florists are on strike. Aren't nuns allowed to read newspapers? Anyway, it's none of your business. Which ward is my wife in? That's all you need to tell me.'

Shortly after, in a scene that must have been very moving, my father blew his boozy breath in my face for the first time.

Five minutes later, maybe ten. Sister Philomena in the corridor, barking at my father: 'Where do you think you're going with that child?'

Me in his arms.

'It's my son, I'll take him wherever I like.'

'Mr Verhulst, he was only born this morning.'

'He's my son. If you want kids of your own to boss around, chuck your wimple over the hedge and hike up your dress, the rest'll take care of itself.' And he carried me out the door.

It had stopped raining – this extenuating detail was always mentioned when telling the story – and my father laid me in the postbag on the front of his bike and rode off to all of his favourite pubs to show me to his friends. Of course they knocked it back like animals. Of course I spent my first few hours in scandalous cigarette smoke and noise. Of course every passing hour saw him less and less able to keep his bike straight. And of course, very late that night, my father delivered me back to the maternity hospital, where my worried mother must have been close to a total cardiac arrest. All of the board members of whatever the club is for the protection of children would undoubtedly raise their eyebrows on hearing these details. I think the story's out and out fantastic. An accident couldn't have been more welcome and there must be plenty of wanted, precisely planned children who had to make do with less of a reception.

The fag shop opened.

I knew that soon, when my child was born, I wouldn't go to as much trouble as my father. And I definitely wouldn't sing. And if I got drunk later that day – which I doubted, but you can't predict everything – it certainly wouldn't be to celebrate its arrival.

Maybe it would be stillborn after all, and I had been worried about nothing the whole time. Maybe a blood test would still prove that it was somebody else's. Hope for the best. Go. And I turned around and walked upstairs, where they were probably nervously awaiting my return.

A Folklorist's Delight

I'd already looked at her the way you look at a lover you'll never see again and I wondered if she'd felt it. The look in her eyes when they met mine could have been dotage, but just as easily sorrow. Maybe her dementia had thrown her back to the crudest form of intelligence, intuition, and she grasped that I would soon be driving home with a lump in my throat, that I'd come to say goodbye, that I was someone who had loved her and been loved by her. A figure from her misty past. But who exactly?

I'd noticed months before that she'd stopped addressing people by name. That way no one had to correct her and she didn't need to be reminded that she was forgetting everything and could no longer tell her children from her grandchildren or even her great-grandchildren. I understood. In my own way, I was struggling with the same confusion. This woman, this shrivelled malodorous little creature, was my grandmother. But if anyone had been my mother, she was it. That was how I would keep her in my heart and that was how I would carry her too, the day I shouldered her coffin next to our Girder, who I saw more as a brother than an uncle.

I refuse to pronounce the poetic name of the old people's home where she was supposed to fade away with dignity. I'd always thought of the names of old people's homes as sarcasm. The home I ended up in as a teenager after driving a foster family up the wall was called 'Spring Meadows', and you could draw a direct line from there to the names of the old folks' homes. The room my grandmother had moved into, the place where lots of her predecessors had undoubtedly died, measured nine by twelve. It stank and I couldn't bear it. I always took her to the cafeteria. Not that she was easy to boss around. First she had to study me carefully, judging whether or not I was trustworthy. After all, I could be anyone and could have hatched a plan to kidnap her. Or rob her. Under her bed she kept the cigar box with the Belgian coins that had become worthless since the introduction of the euro, a treasure she admired every night before going to sleep. It was a shame it didn't produce music when she opened the lid.

'Come on, Nan, we're going to go have a drink in the cafeteria. It's on me.'

And then we'd shuffle down the corridor arm in arm. It seemed endless and full of beds you were afraid might be occupied by someone growing cold under a sheet, ready to be rolled to the washroom, sprayed down and perfumed for a final date in the morgue. And there was always a nurse in the corridor who'd try to soft-soap my grandmother. 'Hi, Maria, you're in luck today, I see. Such a handsome young man to take you for a walk. You get them in, you do . . .' But she was oblivious. The puerile banter was lost on her. She no longer answered with the pride the nurse had tried to evoke, explaining that I was her grandson. She just shuffled her endless path by my side, past bin bags full of nappies, wordless.

The cafeteria was a brick breviary, it always gave a nod to the church calendar. This time there were yellow ribbons and painted eggs suspended from the ceiling to indicate that Easter was on its way, and I wondered whether my grandmother was an exemplary OAP when it came to crafts. I pointed at an egg that had been painted black. 'Did you make that?' She didn't know. It wasn't the kind of thing you'd want to remember. How cruel, being forced to make knick-knacks for an Easter you might not live to see. I ordered a cherry beer for her and a coffee for myself. I rolled a cigarette, hoping she'd comment on it, but there was no response. In the old days she cracked up laughing when she saw me rolling a cigarette. Roll-ups, that was something for fishermen, as far as she was concerned.

'What's it like here?'

No reaction. She put the glass to her lips and took a big mouthful. A few months earlier and she would have asked me where I lived, and I would have lied, because these days it took me three hours to drive from my house to the old people's home. The name of my village wouldn't have rung a single bell, and the name of the remote region in which it was located would have been just as unknown. She would have asked me how it was going at school and I would have answered, good, it's going well at school, I got great marks at Christmas. And three minutes later she would have asked me the same thing again, and again things would have been going well at school. She wouldn't have noticed that I was a little old for a schoolboy and I discounted the possibility of her vaguely thinking I'd become a teacher. Now and then I saw her looking at me in between questions, peering intently, and I realized that she was wondering whether I was her son or grandson. I've played that role sometimes, the role of my father. It came naturally and did me good to see how happy she was to realize that she'd been mistaken: her son wasn't dead, he was sitting right in front of her. He'd shaved off his moustache, that had confused her. By this time several of her children were making the chrysanthemum nurseries good money, and those who were left had to play double roles. But in this phase she didn't ask me anything any more. Goodbye, questions. Goodbye, language. Goodbye, communication. She stared into space and drank her cherry beer.

During the last years of her life there was one person who had grown terribly fond of my grandmother. Marieken. Marieken had Down's syndrome and was the daughter of someone who, on her deathbed, had made the nurses promise to look after her daughter, who she had taken to the home with her so that she could watch over her until her last breath. Marieken herself was already well into her fifties, but much too young to live in an old people's home. My grandmother didn't want anything to do with this peculiar creature who wouldn't budge from her side. 'That loon!' she said. Apparently the senile still feel a distinction from other forms of mental disturbance, and she rated her own forgetfulness higher than Marieken's comical brainwaves. Marieken's behaviour was typical of Down's syndrome, at least if jealousy and sexual obsession are typical of Down's syndrome. It stuck in her throat that other residents got visitors, and she always sat down at the tables around which families had gathered for one more reunion. If I was sitting in the cafeteria with my grandmother, Marieken always joined us, and in the end I got more conversation out of Marieken than I did out of my grandmother. Marieken wanted to have sex with me. There was nothing surprising about that. Marieken wanted to have sex with every man who showed up on Sundays to dutifully hand a box of chocolates and a bunch of flowers to a family member.

'See what a loon she is!'

But if I explained to Marieken that I already had a girlfriend, she seemed to understand my refusal and didn't take it so personally: someone must have told her at some stage that a man and a woman choose each other for an eternal eternity, amen, and never have anything on the side. Sometimes I forgot that Marieken wasn't really a relative: she'd become one of the family and I always brought her a chocolate bar she scoffed like a pig. I was familiar with the association some people make between sex and chocolate. It didn't apply to me, but in that regard Marieken was a carnival attraction for any pop scientist. She could stuff a pound of milk chocolate into her crooked mouth without batting an eyelid; her liver was undoubtedly a giant pudding that would provide great amusement to the pathologist during her autopsy.

I had decided that this was going to be my last visit. Marieken asked if I'd broken up with my girlfriend and I told her to be quiet. She pouted indignantly, crossed her arms and stuck out her tongue. But I wanted to be alone with my grandmother for a moment, for the last time, in a cafeteria full of leaking geriatrics and whingeing children other visitors had brought with them as compensation or to emphasize that the oldies' lives had been passed on, like batons in the perpetual, apparently pointless relay race everyone clung to in the great regrettability of things. It wasn't even clear to me if she still appreciated my company: she would have sat here silently with anyone. As far as I could tell, I wore her out more than I cheered her up. What was passing through her mind, what kind of thoughts, and how horrible was it for her to have a complete stranger give her a cherry beer? Anyway. If she didn't feel like talking, I did, even if she wasn't going to take in any of it. I told her how grateful I was that she had once secretly called a social worker, Nelly Fockedey, to ask if she could find a foster family for a boy who lived with four drunks, who fell asleep at his school desk because he hadn't come home from the pub with his father until early in the morning, who cleaned up his father's vomit and helped him get undressed. I told her about the girlfriend I was totally crazy about and that it was a pity I'd found it necessary to have a child with someone else before meeting the love of my life. But I'd met her, I couldn't complain. I told her about the deer in the forests around my village, the clouds that paraded past the window at which I wrote my books. I told her about Germany, where I'd been a few days before, and the songs I'd heard on Westdeutscher Rundfunk 5, singing along with my sweetheart. That I was happy and didn't rant on as much. That I didn't drink. That I didn't hit my girlfriend.

But I could just as well have told her other things – a summary of a volleyball game would have left her just as cold. Maybe it was the tablets they carried around here on trays like light refreshments to make life easier for the nursing staff. I couldn't tell. She stared at me as if I was on TV.

Good evening, viewers.

'Anyway,' I said, sitting up straight, 'I'll be off then.' That was the moment we looked at each other and she must have felt that it was for the last time. I thought of the poet Hans Andreus who chased his wife away from his deathbed with the words, 'Just go. I have to do this alone.' That comforted me. She would die without me, I knew that. A moment would come, and an evening seemed appropriate, when an uncle or aunt would call me. They would say that it's really the end now, because that's how we put it, that it's the end. They mean that the rattle in her throat is the creak of the ferryman's boat. And they would ask me if I can come quickly. But I will stare out my window, saying that by the time I arrived my grandmother would have reached her destination as well, and thinking: out there my grandmother is dying. I'll feel like scrapping words from the dictionary in my rage. The next time I see her, her skin will be tight again, tanned, cotton pads in her nose will soak up the telltale first signs of decomposition and a nurse will have stuffed rosary beads in between her stiffened fingers. That was what it would be like. I left. May she go easy.

It *was* an evening when I got the call. From our Girder. He didn't sound like his mother was dying.

'Hey, kid, how's it going? I'm not interrupting anything I hope. You weren't shagging the missus, were you? Otherwise I'll ring back some other time. No? You sure? It's about the right time of night for a shag. I'm not ringing too late, am I? No? Anyhow, what I'm ringing about . . .'

Anyhow, what our Girder was ringing about. He'd been rung up himself, he wasn't exactly sure who by, at least, he hadn't remembered the name, but it was some guy who had something to do with folk-lore. A professor of folklore or something like that. Did I happen to know any folklore professors?

I didn't, no. 'What are you actually calling about?'

'Well, I'm about to tell you, see . . . They've started up a project on drinking songs. They've finally realized that drinking songs are part of our cultural heritage. Or maybe inheritance, whatever. And now they want to collect those songs per region. In dialect. They've started doing their research, you see, probably into where the biggest drunks hang out, and to cut a long story short, they ended up with the Verhulsts. Ha-ha. My question now is, do you remember any of those songs?'

'Not really.'

'What do you mean, not really? Your dad used to sing them the whole day long. How'd it go, that song about cherries, help me here . . .'

'The age of wonders lives on yet, the weather's dry and my cherry's wet.'

'Yes, that's it! You have to help us, lad. We've got to write down the complete lyrics.'

'But I only remember the first two lines.'

'And that song about the whorehouse then?'

'"The White Velvet Lover"?'

'Exactly, "The White Velvet Lover". Kid, your memory is scary. Do you realize that? You've got to help us.'

'Girder, I don't remember those songs any more. The last time I heard them was at Dad's funeral, and even then there were verses I'd forgotten. And that's fuck knows how long ago now.'

'It'll come back. If you just apply yourself, the words will come floating up to the surface. I'm sure of it. What you worrying about? You up for it?'

'What do you mean? Up for what?'

'Singing, for fuck's sake. Those guys are going to put it on CD. For the archives. Wouldn't it be fantastic, you and your Uncle Girder on CD? The Arsendegem Brothers, ha-ha.'

I thought it was perverse. It was an illusion to think that anyone was genuinely interested in ordinary people. The pseudo-scientific basis they needed as an excuse betrayed their feelings of superiority. The researcher is an outsider. Did any professors of folklore join us for tea in the old days? Did they come by to dig into the muck we ate with our bare hands? Did they join us in the pub for a bit of mooning on the pool table when the music and level of drunkenness demanded? Were they prepared to lend a hand when we had to knock someone's teeth down his throat in one of our culturally-very-interesting working-class pubs? Did they have the balls to sling a glass ashtray in somebody's face? Had there ever been an academic who would have sung these songs with us for the fun of it, without thinking of a pres-entation or anything like that? Easy pickings for the entertainment of a self-declared artistic bourgeoisie, that was the masses. The authenticity they strove to achieve. The primitives of the industrialized world and their forefathers. Given half a chance they'd drag the plebs' washing lines into the museums to put their underpants and smoky living rooms on display. You could bet your life on it: just organize a washing-line exhibition and you'd take the whole city by storm, such an original idea. Because the intelligentsia is easily satisfied and even more easily drained of inspiration. But once the exhibition was over, the lower classes would still be low, where they belong. In the 1980s the professors of folklore went into the bush with their tape recorders, begging jungle dwellers to sing them a song. Trying to get the whole world in their archives. They saw someone with a long lip and asked them to flap that lip for the cameras. They pushed their microphones up against a Tibetan's Adam's apple to get a better recording of throat singing. And now they'd set up their recording equipment in the houses I'd been raised in. Drinking songs, for God's sake. I had no problem with those drinking songs being part of the cultural heritage, that was fine, but only if it was a living heritage in which the songs come and go, getting corrupted and absorbed by other songs with other lyrics, far away from a definitive recording that could only be a lie. It was truer to my father to let the songs he'd sung die with him, little by little, a verse at a time. How could those art-mongers constantly ignore the mortality of beauty, a pleonasm if ever I'd heard one?

'Kid, how can you say that? Calling it perverse. You take things too seriously. It'd be a laugh, us two pissed as farts on a CD.'

I said I'd think about it.

'That's more like it. Grab a beer out of the fridge and have a think. I'll get back to you.'

I didn't think about it, assuming the whole episode would pass me by. Tomorrow or the day after, they'd forget their intense interest in folklore and be back in the pub making a more sincere contribution to our cultural heritage. But three days later I had our Herman on the line. Years could pass without me hearing from my family, or them from me, and now I had two uncles ringing me up in one week.

'Kid, Uncle Herman here. You know about it, our Girder rang you earlier this week. Well, we've come up with a solution. We're all going to go see our mum, your nan.'

I didn't get it.

'Your nan's as mad as a hatter, lad. She lives one hundred per cent in the past. Inside her head they still have to invent the Hoover. You get me? If anyone can remember the words of our songs, your nan can. Because she doesn't have to remember, see? It's all fresh in her mind. Let me put it this way: it's all she's got in her memory. So she won't have to dig deep to find it.'

'You're taking the fucklorist to the old fucks' home?'

'Ah, you're with me now.'

'I don't want to be with you, Uncle Herman. I think it's disgusting.'

'What's disgusting about it? We just ask her to sing a couple of dirty songs for us. She'll probably enjoy it. Surely you can't object to your old nan having a bit of fun? Do you realize how miserable it must be for her, stuck in an old folks' home like that? This way she can take her mind off things. And it's all in the name of science.'

I was open to a lot of things in life, but my uncles acting in the name of science was going too far. What's more, I couldn't imagine my grandmother ever having sung those songs herself. That was the point: she had to listen to them, probably against her wishes, when my father was at his most entertaining. I could only assume that for someone senile there must be an enormous difference between active and passive knowledge.

'Do it for your dad, kid, come on.'

'Dad's dead, he doesn't have anything to do with this.'

'Wanker. We wouldn't have had to ask your dad twice. He understood the meaning of the word fun.'

'It's got nothing to do with fun. And anyway, that's emotional blackmail. I'm not going to be part of it, end of story.'

'So you're gonna let us down?'

'If you want to see it that way.'

'I do. You're the family's fucking cultural expert. You make your living off culture, giving readings here, there and everywhere. If *we* want to know how you're doing, we have to look in the paper. But now that we, your own flesh and blood, ask you to do something for us for a change, you think your own culture's perverse and disgusting all of a sudden. You'll have to explain that to me sometime, pal.'

'I don't know that it makes any sense to see Nan again,' I said. 'I've already said goodbye.'

'What you doing saying goodbye? She's still alive. She could live another ten years yet. You never know.'

'She's a vegetable, Uncle Herman! At least when I said goodbye to her, I was able partly, somewhere far away, to say goodbye to the person she used to be. But now she's a complete vegetable. A weak vegetable that's only just hanging on.'

'Do you have vegetables in your back garden?'

'Yes,' I said.

'Do you water them?'

'Yes,' I said, even though it was my girlfriend who watered them.

They had everything ready when I arrived at the old people's home, an hour or so late. They'd converted the cafeteria into a kind of recording studio and parked my grandmother at a small table in the middle in her wheelchair, flanked by microphones. The other oldies – the knitters, dreamers, nose pickers, pipe smokers, tobacco chewers, droolers, hawkers and farters – fully or partially conscious, sat around to observe the shenanigans, and the staff had another excellent enter-tainment programme up and running for the afternoon. The recording equipment didn't make any impression at all on my grandmother. She sat there. Showing the obliviousness with which she submitted to X-rays, as apathetically as she allowed hospital apparatus to be inserted into her body. Like that. That was how she sat there. She breathed and her heart beat. That was about it. This was going to come to nothing.

'Ah, kid, there you are. What kept you so long? We've been sitting here cooling our heels waiting for you.'

'I went to buy a couple of pounds of chocolate for Marieken.'

Marieken was dead. That was easiest for everyone, otherwise she would have just tried to sabotage everything out of jealousy, angry that my grandmother was getting the attention instead of her. If I'd come to visit a bit more often, I'd have at least known she was dead. And now I knew. I shared the chocolate out amongst the oldies, who were waiting like zombies for something to happen. Someone who knew a lot about dials and switches but not much about life – probably a producer – had put a pair of headphones on my grandmother's bony skull. She didn't kick up any kind of fuss: we could have put a flowerpot on her head for all she cared. Any child would have been happy to play with a doll like this: there might not have been much hair left to comb, but they could change nappies till the cows came home.

The gentlemen who wanted to turn the folk into a lore gave each of us a sheet of paper and asked us to sign it. A formality: it said we renounced all rights to these recordings. Our Girder signed immediately. He'd never cared two hoots about the contents of a document. 'I've never had any rights in this country and I'm happy to renounce any I'm supposed to have. That way they can't bother me.' Our Herman followed his example, regally adding his scrawl under a paragraph of legal mumbo-jumbo. I could have made trouble, but if I was honest about it, I couldn't care less what happened to these recordings, even if I found out afterwards they'd turned them into hit singles and made a fortune. Fine by me.

'So. We going to start?'

A nurse warned the watching oldies to be quiet, they were about to start recording, and the occupants of several wheelchairs really did seem to believe that something spectacular was about to happen.

'We're going to make a CD, Mrs Verhulst. A CD with your voice on it. Isn't that wonderful?'

My grandmother didn't know what that was, a CD. Of course she didn't, she'd never held one in her hand. If she was lucky she might have heard someone mention one once, like she'd heard people talk about the Internet.

'All you have to do is sing some rude songs. Old-style drinking songs. It doesn't matter which ones.'

Of course my grandmother didn't break out of the cocoon dementia had woven around her, she didn't move a muscle or give us any clues as to whether she was still in touch with the world in which we had known her. Our Herman suggested we start with the lines we remembered. Nan would then, maybe, enthused by it all, simply start singing along and we'd be on our way. Given that he didn't have any alternatives, the producer thought this was an excellent idea.

'Kid, will you start? Do "The Cherry Picker's Song" first, your dad's favourite.'

I couldn't do it. I might have been able to if I'd knocked back a couple of beers first, and when I said so, they were convinced I'd handed them the key to drinking songs. Of course you couldn't sing them sober. It was impossible. It shouldn't even be allowed. Boozing songs required booze. It was that simple. We should have thought of it before. We had struck on the essence of the drinking song and that too

182

seemed only logical to the scientists, who were even willing to pick up the tab. Now they were talking. Four beers later, realizing that I didn't have the patience to wait until we were all pissed, I brought my mouth up close to the microphone and sang.

'The age of wonders lives on yet, the weather's dry and my cherry's wet.'

So, we'd made a start.

Now we just had to come up with the next line. We remembered how the tune went, so we started humming and kept it up through the whole song. Maybe this was the way to break open our memories, and my grandmother's.

'We're not drunk enough yet,' Girder concluded. 'Another thirty, thirty-five beers and we'll be singing all these songs without even thinking.'

Now and then I looked at my grandmother, a piece of time's effrontery, and it occurred to me that it would be typical for us if she was now sitting there dead in her wheelchair with the headphones on her liver-spotted skull. Having died quietly while we were getting stuck into it and winding ourselves up over the words of a song, surrounded by her drunken sons. But she was still alive, technically.

The hours passed, the old people lost their interest in the promised spectacle and were wheeled off to the dining room for their mash and bread crusts dipped in soup. Their syrups and their pills. They put my grandmother's daily pill on her tongue too, like the host in the old days, and she swallowed just as meekly and with the same blind trust.

A family in black appeared at the reception desk – soon they'd get to rack their brains over the redistribution of goods and chattels – and we chewed over our filthiest and smuttiest words, trying in vain to fit them into a song. The producer checked his watch and started worrying, he too was growing older. They started to pack up and put away the microphones. Not one of us had donated his voice to science.

'A real shame,' mused Girder, 'I would have loved that, us on a CD.'

'We think it's a pity too. But thanks for trying, for going to all this trouble.' The producer. You could see he didn't mean it. He'd wasted his time.

'Oh well, at least we got a free drink out of it. And it wasn't that much of a chore. It got us out the door for once and we saw our old mum again while we were at it.'

They shook hands and exchanged vacuum-sealed sentences, and the friends of ordinary people left the old folks' home to head off to their next task, filming a folk dance perhaps. We wanted another beer but the nurse wouldn't give us any more. The cafeteria was closing, the residents all had to be showered and they were a little confused because of the disruption of their daily schedule. In a few minutes they would wheel my grandmother to the dining room. She was out of kilter too, according to the nurse. I looked into her eyes, trying to find something to hold on to, but it was clear, we had already said goodbye to each other. When they came to get her, I waved as if she was a toddler and she smiled. She smiled, out of the blue, and said, perfectly audibly:

'The cock crowed once, the cock crowed twice, I started feeling very nice.'

Exactly! That was the next line of 'The Cherry Picker's Song', how could we have forgotten it?

'It's enough to drive you to drink!' said our Herman.

An Uncle to the Boy

It's obvious he's bored. He tears up beer mats and makes little animals from the foil his chocolate was wrapped in. I show him how to use the beer mats to build a house of cards instead, but no one can convince me I've made a positive contribution to his education by doing so. Humanity has built too much already. If his generation doesn't get started on the demolition, we'll be in serious trouble. But after getting discouraged by a series of collapsing houses, he loses his concentration and, above all, his patience and pulls on the handle of the fruit machine, which bewitches and delights him with its riffs and thousands of lights. For now he's content to just pull the handle, still believing that the machine is reacting to his actions, that he's lord and master of this little bit of paradise. He sees a connection between his tugs on the handle and the flashing of the lights, a connection that only exists in his mind and lasts until someone else chucks a coin into the machine. Then he learns that anyone who pays what it takes can be God, if only briefly. His little brain almost overloads watching the numbers race back and forth, making little tunes play. It comes as no surprise when he, after being forced to move to make room for someone who wants to try his luck, comes up to me and asks, 'Daddy, can I have a go on the machine?' It's a fruit machine, a source of comfort for grown-ups who like a bit of entertainment with their impoverishment, and not appropriate for children. But not wanting to tell him that it's a machine for grown-ups, I search for a reason he'll understand. As a kid I always thought it was stupid the way people always told me that things were for grown-ups, not me.

'That's a machine for grown-ups, kiddo.'

He puts the straw in his mouth and blows bubbles into his Coke until that starts to bore him too.

'How long now, Dad?'

'How long to what, son?'

'To Mum.'

Five more hours. He's got a lot of hours in front of him, too many to count. His time is still overflowing, so he doesn't know the meaning of an hour. Seconds, weeks, hours, metres, litres, none of it means a thing to him, even if he pretends otherwise. There are no measurements for fantasy. He loves his mother. Later I'll deliver him back to her door and he'll fly into her arms, the arms in which I suffocated, and let her hug him tight and cover him with kisses. This weekend he finally asked me. It wasn't a question; he said, 'You don't love Mummy.' And I said, 'No, I don't love your mummy.' He must have found that unbelievable, someone not loving his mummy, amazed that something like that could even be possible. I wonder what the experts think of that, what it must have done to his psychology. 'But I do love you,' I added, mainly to avoid worrying him. He doesn't know that, like him, I'll be glad when I finally hand him back to his mother. I'm his father and I should feel like a father, but only seeing him once a fortnight doesn't tear me up. I never miss him when he's not around and it wouldn't feel like a punishment if I didn't see him for a whole year. Fathers are for every day, they never take a day off. When he is around, I find it pleasant enough, usually. I do my best to make it enjoyable for him, providing, together with my girlfriend, a way of life he can accept or reject as he pleases. I see that he's not being brought up the way I'd prefer, but it's easy for me to talk, I'm not bringing him up. I'm a kind of uncle for my own son, full of energy when he comes to visit, energy he drains out of me in two days, so that I'm glad when I can finally put him back into his mother's arms and flop down jelly-like on the sofa. I'd rather adopt a stray dog.

Do I love the kid? You need to have made a choice for each other before you can talk of love. So, no. I know what love is. My girl and I love each other like rare fools. I almost never encounter them, others who love each other, even though it's not difficult at all. I know that now. Love is easy. And the boy? God, I wish him well. There are many paths he can take in life and I'd like to be his road map. Is that pathetic? So be it. I feel something when I see him laughing as he gallops his horse around the merry-go-round, it moves me. And my heart is wrenched when he sits up sobbing in bed because the ghosts come out whenever an adult leaves him alone in the room. If that's a kind of love, fine by me.

My girl has gone to work and I miss her. I think he's more attached to my girlfriend than he is to me. I can't blame him.

'I like it more when Nathalie's here.'

'Me too, son, me too.'

With her here we'd play hide-and-seek in the wood, follow the wild boars' droppings, study the beavers' dams, check whether the hawks have already built this years' nests on the ledges of the cliffs. But without my girl I didn't have the energy for so much cheerfulness, and pushed him into the car and drove to Arsendegem. God knows what I was thinking. We'd already played his favourite CD of demented children's songs twice before we even reached the cemetery, where I told him, 'Kid, this is where your grandfather's buried.' There was another voice no one heard, saying, 'Dad, look, this is your grandson!' He already had a grandfather and he was a bit shocked to discover another one, buried under a marble slab. Gradually an awareness of death was seeping into his brain, the flat rabbits on the road made sure of that. And he could already act it quite well, being dead. He's a wiz, for example, at playing dead when it's time to eat. Now he's got a formidable opponent at his game and has to admit the superiority of this unknown grandfather.

He actually looks like my father, I thought while wandering over the cemetery with him, checking whether my mother had taken up residence yet. Just to be on the safe side, I read the names on the headstones too, I wasn't convinced I would recognize her photo. But I didn't find her. Afterwards I took him to the pub to introduce him to my uncles, confident they'd be there propping up the bar.

We're still sitting here waiting and he's getting bored.

'Well, fuck me dead, who do we have here?'

Here they are: Herman and Girder. It's taken long enough.

'What cat dragged you in? Is this your kid? He's the spitting image of our P., two peas in a pod for God's sake.'

He stares at the strangers with big eyes, baffled by their accents.

'What you call him?'

'Yuri.' As ugly as a name can be. His mother chose it. Yuri – sounds like something for a car. An Opel Yuri.

'Yuri. Nice name. Hey, Yuri, shake hands with your Uncle Girder . . . Okay, let's have some drinks here!'

I can't, I tell him. I've got to drive.

'You'll have to come up with a better excuse than that, mate, the one time we get to see you.' And a beer was plonked down in front of me. More to the point, there's a second beer there before I've had a chance to have a good look at the first one. If the kid's mum smells booze on my breath when I give him back, I can start looking for a lawyer.

'Take it easy, guys, I have to take the kid back to his mother's in a couple of hours. I have to look a bit respectable, huh?' But by then they're already on their fourth.

'Dad, can I have a go on the machine?'

He knows what I think about it. He's just trying it on because there are other people here now. I turn him down flat.

'Haven't you got a few cents for the kid to have a go on the fruit machine? What's that about? Here, lad, Uncle Herman will let you have a go on the fruit machine.'

I hate the triumphant look in the boy's eyes. It's the look of a whore, someone who's ready to give his affection to the highest bidder.

'What are you doing?' I say to our Herman. 'If I say he's not allowed, why should you let him?'

'Don't be stupid, kid. So what if he has a bit of fun on the fruit machine? You get out of the wrong side of bed or what?'

'No, I didn't get out of the wrong side of bed, but I don't want my kid playing those poker machines, and especially not at his age. I think I can rightly say that poker machines aren't good for anyone, and if I'm not mistaken you know that best of all.'

'You just come here to moan or what?'

'I came here because I felt like seeing you guys.'

'I hadn't noticed.'

I haven't been one of them for a long time and the proof is that they've started talking to me in something that's supposed to pass for standard Dutch, the same way they speak to my son. Even though I know how stuck-up they find it. I no longer speak my old dialect. I occasionally burst into it when I'm angry or drunk. Rarely, in other words. Extremely rarely. I'm not one of them, but I'd like to be. I wish I could show my loyalty or my love, whatever you want to call those feelings.

'Tell us, how are things with you?'

I'm happy, but that sounds so terrible. As if I'm ashamed of my own happiness. Earning a living from something I do with so much pleasure, owning a house I wouldn't give up for a fortune, having a girlfriend without neuroses who loves me and, hard to believe, doesn't want kids with me, a girlfriend I never need to swear at or thump. I've got fire insurance, a car, a chainsaw and a frying pan. And I pay national insurance contributions without begrudging it at all. I couldn't be more of a defector. What could I possibly talk to my uncles about?

'Good,' I say, 'everything's fine, thanks. And here? How's it hanging?'

I said that last bit because I thought it was the kind of expression they'd like, but it falls flat. I sound like a ventriloquist's dummy.

'What's that? How's it hanging? They say that down your way? That's daft.'

'Don't they say that round here?'

Our Potrel's is hanging just dandy, as always, but that's as far as it goes. They've grown old. Older than I thought they'd ever be. Older than they ever wanted.

'Fag?'

I admit to being in the middle of my umpteenth feeble attempt to give up.

'Cancer'll get you anyway.'

That's true. I puff my way through four in a row, thinking, the kid's going to stink of cigarettes when I take him back to his mother. I'll tell her: cancer will get him anyway.

There he stands, tugging on the handle of his dream machine. He looks happy. That machine was the childhood bliss I wanted to deprive him of.

'What's that on that fruit machine next to the kid?' I look at our Girder.

'What do you mean, what's that?'

'You know what I'm talking about. That glass. What's in that glass?'

'That's a diesel. You're not going to tell me you don't know what a diesel is. You used to know what diesel is.'

'You telling me my son's drinking diesel?'

'He likes it!'

'Girder, the boy's five years old.'

'So what? Your dad gave you diesels when *you* were five.'

'Maybe that's just what I'm getting at, Girder.'

'Don't get your knickers in a twist, lad, there's hardly any beer in it. It's three-quarters Coke. And to be honest, if anything's bad for you, it's Coke. All that sugar.'

I take the boy's diesel away, annoying him immensely. He'll definitely make a show of not touching the strawberry drink I replace it with. The little shit. He won't eat vegetables, you have to ram them down his throat like they do with geese at a foie gras farm. But his fussiness doesn't extend to a glass of diesel.

'Nowadays they're already on drugs at the age of twelve, and you're sitting here kicking up God knows what kind of fuss over a harmless glass of diesel.'

'I don't want to know, Girder, end of story.'

'Come on, lad, what did they do to you in the old days in all those homes and foster families?'

I ask myself the same question.

'I don't know you any more.'

If it's any comfort to him, often I don't know myself either.

I have to remind myself that this is just the tone they use when talking, it hasn't got anything to do with them being warm or cold. Cuddly is just something they've never done. It's only from a distance that people might think we're not crazy about each other.

We should have sussed it: the boy has been playing that damn fruit machine for half an hour with just fifty eurocents. Not exactly normal. When our Herman goes to see what's going on, the mystery is solved: there's fifteen hundred euros lying in the tray. And every time Yuri pulls the handle, more coins come clattering down, pleasing him no end. Weird we didn't hear anything.

'One thousand five hundred euros – God almighty, I haven't got that much out of that machine in my whole life. Well done, Yuri. Give us all some, this is something we have to celebrate.'

I don't want any of it and I want the boy going home with that amount of money even less. Our Herman can keep the profits, it was his investment. Let him buy himself a beer or two.

'You gone mad? That's God knows how much money. You could buy a mountain of toys for the lad with that.'

'No way. Before you know it, he'll start thinking you can actually make money off those machines.'

'There's fifteen hundred euros lying there, dimwit. What's that? Has he made money off it or what?'

'It's your money and that's all there is to it.'

'If you insist.' And he gives the kid a fifty-euro note. 'A little pocket money from Uncle Herman.'

'Harrar!' says our Girder.

'What?'

'Harrar, I tell you.'

'Where's Harrar?'

'On the radio, moron, the answer to the quiz.'

We used to put coins in this pub's jukebox – now they just play the radio.

'You got a phone on you, kid? I need to call the radio urgently.'

I give him my telephone and the whole pub shuts up. Our Girder paces back and forth with the telephone, constantly bumping into a wall of engaged signals. They turn the radio up louder and Girder gives a disappointed scowl when a quicker caller gets to give their answer on the radio. Someone with four children, a horticulturalist by trade, happily married and with walking as his hobby. 'Goebbels,' he guesses, and that's too bad for him, the DJ switches to the next contestant.

Our Girder is suddenly on the radio, he's got through.

'Good afternoon, who do I have on the line?'

'Karel,' says our Karel. 'Karel Verhulst, Girder to his friends.'

'Good afternoon, Karel, tell the listeners something about your-self.'

'Humph, er . . . I've got a whole bunch of kids with different women who all took off ages ago. I don't work. Booze is my fate and the joy of my life and hobbies are for idiots.'

'Original, Karel, original, and do you also know the answer to today's question? I'll just repeat it for the listeners: *If only because of the film, it is reasonably well known that Blondi was the name of Adolf Hitler's* dog. We, however, are asking for the name of the German shepherd the Führer chose to impregnate Blondi. It's not easy, I know that.'

'Harrar,' he barks, because he's had to restrain himself from giving the answer all this time. And it's true, Harrar is the correct answer. Our Potrel can visit the sponsor's video shop to pick up a DVD or video to the value of twenty-five euros.

'So, Karel, do you already have an idea which film you'll be taking home with you?'

'Oh, something with lots of nude chicks in it. *Pussylick III* or something like that. Or otherwise an animated film with Bambi in it.'

'Well, I wish you lots of viewing pleasure. Thanks for your call and, once again, congratulations on your correct answer.'

'Holy moly,' says our Herman, 'was it a repeat?'

'How'd you know that?'

I have to head off. Yuri has to be back at his mum's on time, he really mustn't be late.

'What? Already? You only just got here.'

Either way, I have to get going.

'Can I get a ride off you? You can drop me at the video shop, if that's okay. Then I can pick up my prize.'

Fine by me. Of course he can have a ride.

My car is not the kind real men drive, but it goes. And it's all paid for.

'That your wheels?'

'It's practical.'

'Nice car. Looks like you're doing all right.'

'Not bad. I can't complain. How come you haven't got a car?'

'If I buy a car, the bailiff takes it off me inside a week. That's why I don't even think about getting a job. They deduct everything from my pay.'

'Ah, I get it. That's why you've got so much time to study German shepherds.'

'That bothers you, doesn't it? Harrar: me knowing something like that. But you can relax, they've taken away my civil rights, so I'm not allowed to vote.'

I should tell him that he's not allowed to smoke in the car either, that it's much too small a space for that filthy reek and the kid shouldn't be forced to breathe in other people's smoke, but I restrain myself. It's too late anyway. I'm better off seizing the opportunity myself and lighting one up. I put on a CD.

'What are you putting on now? That's for old people, lad.'

'Roy Orbison.'

'I know it's Roy Orbison, but don't tell me you still listen to that.'

'Roy is unique. All his numbers are complete. He doesn't need to play his choruses three times in a row to finish a song.'

'Twat.' And he rummages through the glovebox, looking for something more appealing and not finding it. Suddenly a photo on a CD cover grabs his attention: a beauty in bed.

'What's this?' He shows me the CD.

'Anthony and the Johnsons,' I say.

'Good-looking chick!'

'That's no chick, Girder.'

'No, of course not, what else is it? Look at her giving me the eye from that CD cover. It's like she's calling out to me, "Come on, Girder, give it to me." That babe's been waiting her whole life for me.'

'Maybe, but it's a man dressed up as a woman.'

'A nancy boy?'

'Put it on. It's worth a listen.'

'What do you take me for? You think I'm going to sit here and listen to dirty homo music? I'd rather shit in my pants. We'll get by without.'

When we finally reach the video shop, he asks me to wait for a sec till he's out again. He'll be right back.

It hasn't gone the way I expected, I think while drumming my fingers on the steering wheel. I should have come without the boy, so I could get drunk with my uncles, not stopping until we were singing and sobbing our mutual declarations of love. I'm the one who acted like a stranger, the stranger I may well have become, and I'd been a prig for not wanting to talk about my happiness for fear they might not be interested. They would have been glad to hear it was going so well.

He's come out of the video shop and signals for me to wind down the window.

'Here,' he says, 'this is for the kid.'

It's the animated film with Bambi in it.

'Shall I drop you home?'

'I'll find my own way, thanks. Look after yourself, and don't do anything I wouldn't do.'

'You neither, Girder, you neither. Bye.'

My son waves Girder goodbye for a very long time. Now we'll have to sit in the car together for a good hour and I don't actually know what to say to him. He could make things easy for me by falling asleep, but that's not his style. I ask him if it's been a fun weekend, and I see his reflection nodding in the rear-view mirror. He's nodding because it's easy that way, he thinks it's what I expect of him.

'Is it far?'

'We'll be at Mummy's soon. One more hour.'

'Shall we sing a song?' he asks.

'Have you learnt a new song at school?'

'No. Uncle Girder just taught it to me.'

'I don't want to hear those songs, Yuri. I know Uncle Girder and his songs and they're no good. Think of something else.'

'But it's a song about birds!'

'Maybe it is, son, but I don't feel like it. Anyway, singing in the car is dangerous, I have to concentrate on the traffic.'

Another hour, I think. Just one short hour.

'Dad?'

'Yes, son?'

'I've got to piss.'

'What?'

'I've got to piss.'

'You mean you have to do a pee. Wee-wee.'

'Yes, Dad.'

'I don't want to hear the word "piss" again, you hear me? It's a dirty word for dirty people.'

The service station is crawling with fathers and mothers whisking their kids off to the toilets. The cubicle doors are open, you can see the kids doing their best with their pants around their ankles while a parent looks on approvingly or intervenes when things get out of hand. What am I doing here? In the old days I at least got a hint of a holiday feeling at a service station. Just one hour to go, I think, while my son amuses everyone by standing there completely independently and singing a song about birds while pissing into the urinal.